STEP-BY-STEP

MIRACLES

Shira Block

STEP-BY-STEP MIRACLES

A Practical Guide to Achieving Your Dreams

KENSINGTON BOOKS

KENSINGTON BOOKS are published by

Kensington Publishing Corp.
850 Third Avenue
New York, NY 10022

First Kensington Trade Paperback Printing: July, 1995

ISBN: 0-8217-4990-0

Printed in the United States of America

With love and gratitude
to my friends and family
whose support and
encouragement have
allowed me to reach for
my dreams

CONTENTS

ACKNOWLEDGMENTS

To you Kathy Missell for your encouragement and faith in me. You have been a guiding light on the path of my life's work. To Deborah Mutschler for inspiring structure and flow in this work as well as in my life. To Ilana Katz for your technical contribution as well as for your continual encouragement, friendship, and support. To Sandy Satterwhite for the direction you have given me as well as for the many introductions and opportunities. And to Taylor Brooke for your fine-tuning.

I would also like to express my gratitude to friends, family, and students whose constant insights and challenges propel my own learning and growth.

FOREWORD

I have spent most of my life exploring various avenues to true happiness. During my journey I have been blessed with wonderful teachers and guides who have shown me ways to experience profound joy, success, and peace. The decision to compile and share the basics of what I have learned stems from my being thankful for having crossed paths with these enlightened beings, as well as the desire to give to others what has been given to me.

This book is a result of years of study and joy, and is comprised of techniques from the many disciplines that have accelerated growth in all areas of my life, as well as in the lives of others.

As you read each chapter you will be reminded of concepts that you have always known but never learned how to put to use. There will also be ideas that are new to you. In both cases, give yourself a chance to absorb the information by reviewing the principles slowly. The exercises provided in most chapters are designed to help you integrate these concepts in all areas of your life.

I offer this body of information to you in the knowledge that as you experience the Step-by-Step Method, you will begin to see life-enhancing changes. Continue to use the Step-by-Step Method and you will experience what many would call miracles.

Shira Block

Part I

FOUNDATION

FOR CHANGE

1

CLAIMING YOUR FUTURE

Unlike those moments in cooking when you find you have to run out to the store for missing ingredients, life does not require last-minute shopping. You already have inside you all the ingredients you'll ever need to be happy, successful, and independent of the economy, your friends, your spouse, your boss, and other outside forces.

The Step-by-Step Method described in this book will show you how to access and fully utilize the vast internal resources that can enable you to live in greater happiness, prosperity, and success. Unfortunately, many of us use these internal resources to create results that mirror our unhappy or unsuccessful past. But by using the Step-by-Step Method with focus and intention, you will learn how to effectively use them to create the future of your dreams.

As you strive for a richer life, you will find yourself coming face to face with the particular beliefs that determine how much joy, love, prosperity, or success you believe you can—or deserve—to have. The Step-by-Step Method will teach you how to expand your beliefs in order to allow more of what you really *want* into your life. Only you can change yourself. The Step-by-Step Method merely gives you the tools to make the immediate yet far-reaching beneficial changes in your life that only you can make.

It is true that self-esteem is a result of past conditioning, of the many and varied experiences of childhood, adolescence, and adulthood. However, this does not mean you must remain a victim of your past. You can at any moment acknowledge why you're where you are in life, why you feel the way you do; and you can make beneficial changes. You should never ignore the impact your past has had on your present. Acknowledge the past, acknowledge the present—and then claim the future!

The Step-by-Step Method will help you design and claim your future by:

1. Identifying the way your mind works and teaching you to benefit from that knowledge
2. Pinpointing the process you currently use to achieve results in your life, then teaching you how to make easy shifts in that process to attain the results you *really* want
3. Outlining principles that may have worked against you in the past, and showing you how they can work for you in the present and future
4. Showing you how you process information
5. Teaching step-by-step techniques that will bring greater success in all areas of your life, from relationships to career to financial security.

The exercises provided throughout the book will help determine what has been blocking you, aid you in eliminating those old habits and beliefs, and guide you to your goals. You will learn how to craft a life that is true to your dreams. Take the time to do each exercise with reflection. You will be surprised by the discoveries you make. When you feel particularly resistant to a certain exercise, take note and examine exactly how—and what—you feel. What you learn will be a powerful aid on your journey.

The Step-by-Step Method is easy to use and completely within your grasp. All you need to do is open your heart, do the exercises step-by-step, and be prepared for miracles.

2

UNDERSTANDING YOURSELF AND THE WAY YOU LEARN

What we are today comes from our thoughts of yesterday,
And our present thoughts build on our
life of tomorrow.

—Buddha

In order to make permanent changes that will improve your life, you must understand how your mind works and how you learn. Many disciplines set forth theories explaining these processes, and although each discipline employs its own terminology, the same theme runs through all. Once you understand this theme, you will have the power to make dramatic shifts in the way you think and behave.

The learning mind can be divided into three parts:

1. Ego
2. Conscious
3. Subconscious

The ego is our personality. It is the net through which we filter life's experiences, perceive humor, elation, anger, and pain. The conscious mind, in processing the ego's experiences, creates generalizations which are then taught to the subconscious. The subconscious mind demonstrates that it has received its lesson by seeking experiences that will reinforce it. This means that whatever we have learned through experience, no matter how outdated, no matter what we intellectually know as true, our subconscious has embraced a belief system, and continually seeks out experiences to validate it.

The ego has the experience and makes a judgment as to whether it was positive or negative. The conscious mind processes the experience, forms a generality, and teaches the generality to the subconscious. The subconscious mind, takes the information from the conscious mind, and creates behaviors that reinforce those beliefs and theories.

This process is exemplified in the following case studies.

Susan R.: Susan was involved in another unhealthy relationship she wished to end. She noticed that the relationships always started out well, but began to deteriorate after the first few months. She could not understand why she was constantly attracted to the wrong men, to men who did not appreciate her.

After long discussions, Susan determined that when she was growing up her father spent very little time with the family.

Her ego had experienced an absentee father. Her conscious mind generalized that any men in her life were, and would be, inattentive. Her subconscious mind then sought out experiences to validate the belief system. Consequently, when Susan met a man who tended to be somewhat aloof or emotionally distant, her subconscious believed that person was a potentially correct partner for her.

Becoming aware of her programmed belief system allowed Susan to reteach her subconscious mind using methods you will learn in the following chapters. As she slowly changed her deep-seated belief system, her life changed. Each change in her experience further reinforced the new belief, making it stronger.

Elliot M.: Elliot is a member of an on-going prosperity workshop in Boston. His parents are loving and caring people who encouraged him to be at his best in all things. He excelled in school and has a Ph.D. in physics. His home life is stable and happy. He has a wife and daughter. However, a negative pattern exists in Elliot's life: He regularly loses jobs. Over the past ten years he has been fired four times. When things are going well at work he sabotages his success by fighting with his boss, missing a crucial deadline, or making inexcusable errors.

With support from the other members of the prosperity group, Elliot was able to trace the origins of his belief about working and job loss to his teen years. His parents had always impressed upon him the importance of doing his best, and Elliot took their advice to heart. At the age of sixteen he got his first job at a local drug store. Like any new employee, he went through a period in which he was learning the job. During that probationary time, however, he was very hard on himself; with each mistake he made, he felt more insecure about his competence. He was sure he would be fired. This created an enormous amount of anxiety in him. He wouldn't allow himself to learn the job properly, and so came to believe that his "best" was just not adequate. Eventually he was fired.

With each job he then took, Elliot experienced the same type of anxiety. This, and his corresponding behavior, served to strengthen his belief that he was incompetent. Over time, he built up an arsenal of facts and stories that "proved" this was so.

As an adult, Elliot continued to be a failure to subconsciously validate his vision of himself. But by identifying his beliefs, he has been able to make changes in his workplace behavior. This new behavior taught his subconscious that he is competent and potentially prosperous.

The first step in making improvements in your life is identifying your ingrained beliefs. The following exercise is geared toward understanding the nature of those beliefs. It will take approximately thirty minutes and will give you valuable information about yourself and the way you have categorized your experiences.

EXERCISE: IDENTIFYING THE CULPRIT

In list form, write down the areas in your life with which you feel dissatisfied. (Not having enough money, unhappy relationships, being taken advantage of, poor health, etc.). After you have compiled your list, take one area and list several different times during which you experienced a particular dissatisfaction. The circumstances may not be exactly the same in terms of details, but they may have felt the same or have had the same end result. For example:

1. Unhappy relationships
   - *a) Your best friend decided not to continue the friendship.*
   - *b) Your partner suddenly broke up with you.*
   - *c) Your boss blames you for everything that goes wrong in the office.*

2. Not enough money
a) You are consistently underpaid.
b) You lose your wallet.
c) You get laid off.
3. Poor health
a) You catch whatever cold or flu is going around.
b) You regularly fall and hurt yourself.

The next step is to make yourself comfortable. Now try to think back to your first unfavorable experience in the area you're checking out. You are looking for clues about why this first incident occurred. Do not push yourself. Try not to create stress about remembering. If nothing comes to mind at first, do not worry. You can always move on to a different area and come back to this one later. Maybe it will not be an experience you choose to recall but something that was taught to you through behavior or words. In Susan, an absentee father created the feeling that she would be unappreciated by men. In Elliot's case, he grew to believe that he was incompetent and could not hold down a job. Identify the nature of your beliefs. Write them down. Defining your beliefs, as Sue and Elliot did, begins to demystify the reasons why things seem to "happen" to you. This is the first step in reteaching yourself new beliefs and behaviors.

Now acknowledge the favorable circumstances in your life, the areas in which you feel satisfied. For example: You have good relationships, good health, a flow of opportunities.

Having completed the previous exercise, you have taken the first step toward understanding the way in which you think. The next step is to fully understand the way in which you receive information. You now know a process whereby the subconscious mind seeks out experiences to validate its belief system. You are about to learn how the subconscious mind does this.

You have been taught that you live life and process information through your five senses. You have been taught to discount impressions you cannot support with "facts." However, you actually relate, form opinions, gain knowledge, pick relationships, make decisions, and live life through information gained energetically, or through means undetectable by sight, sound, touch, taste, or smell.

Have you ever walked into a room where an argument has recently taken place? With no supporting physical evidence, you can sense the tension and anger. Have you ever driven to work and for no verifiable reason had a feeling of "impending doom"? Have you ever been thinking about a friend to whom you have not spoken recently, and later that day found a message from that friend on your answering machine? If two people are walking down the street side by side, and not touching in any way, are you still able to tell that they are deeply in love? Probably. Emotions are sensed energetically.

The energy that we all put out and receive is sensed through our subconscious minds. This energy acts as a map or a beacon for the subconscious as it seeks out the experiences that allow us to re-create patterns, both positive and negative. In terms of beliefs, like energies attract. When a belief system exists, the subconscious mind seeks out a compatible energy. This is done through vibration frequency that will be explained later on in this chapter. The important thing to note at this time is that our feelings and beliefs are felt by others on a subconscious level. A powerful example of this occurs when you meet someone for the first time and you feel you have known that person all your life, that you are attuned to, and strongly sense, who this person is.

Acknowledging your "gut" feelings strengthens your conscious access to your subconscious mind, which is often referred to as your intuition. The more you act on that intuition the more useful it becomes to you. As you begin to trust your instincts, or feelings, about situations, you will strengthen your intuition, and your subconscious then becomes an invaluable tool for achieving your goals.

Most people can sense on a first meeting whether someone is trustworthy or sincere. Few act on those impressions one hundred percent of the time. How often have you disregarded a feeling and ended up saying, "I should have listened to myself"?

The following exercise will take approximately ten minutes.

It will put you in touch with the fact that you energetically process information every day.

EXERCISE: HOW DID YOU KNOW THAT?

List several circumstances in which you knew information that could not be "proven" through the five senses. For example: You knew who was on the phone before you picked it up. You sensed that a friend could use your help. You felt there was going to be problem at work. You were certain a meeting was going to be canceled.

You now know the way your mind learns, and that you gain energetic or intuitive information along with information received through the five senses. The next step is to understand how this process of intuitive or energetic learning occurs. The basics of this explanation are ancient principles which were written down thousands of years ago and which are now being verified through techniques of modern-day science. Seven of these ancient principles have formed the structure for the Masters of Spirituality and have been utilized as part of the basic teachings on personal empowerment throughout this century. They are called the Seven Hermetic Truths or Principles. These truths offer simple explanations as to how you are able to create your life situations at will, through your own internal power. For our purposes, we will only be discussing three of them. (If you are interested in reading about all seven, please see the recommended reading list at the end of this book.)

PRINCIPLE 1: THE PRINCIPLE OF MENTALISM

This principle states that in our world everything that has been created begins with a thought. There would be no buildings on Main Street if someone had not first thought, This looks like a good place for commercial real estate. What we wear, what we eat, the person we date, absolutely everything we do, no matter how big or small, begins with a thought. When we enter the kitchen to make dinner, the meal is only created after the thought: I think I'll make spaghetti.

This being the case, we cannot have anything, do anything, or be anything unless we conceptualize it. For example, in order for us to experience wealth, we must first see it in our minds. We must at least say to ourselves, "I would like to have more money." If we would like to become involved in a permanent relationship, we must conjure the picture or thought of what we want in our mind. We do not necessarily need to *see* the picture, but we must at least have the feeling, the thought, and know what it is that we want. Unfortunately, past experiences make it easy to see ourselves where we are, having less than we want or need.

The Step-by-Step Method uses the Principle of Mentalism in your favor through cultivating, strengthening, and focusing thoughts. You are going to devote thought and energy into reconditioning and reteaching your subconscious mind. The ultimate goal of this process is to reteach yourself so that you can create a future that exceeds the experiences of the past and can live in abundance.

In his book *Perfect Health,* world-renowned Dr. Deepak Chopra states that the average human being has approximately sixty thousand thoughts a day. Ninety-five percent of those thoughts are the same ones we had yesterday. Since you now know that everything begins with a thought, it is no surprise that each day you re-create your past by thinking the same thoughts as you did the day before, thereby strengthening your current notion of what you can and cannot have. However, your past does not have to equal the future. In the following chapters you will learn how, with ease, to enrich your thoughts and create a new future—a future you have always wanted.

PRINCIPLE 2: THE PRINCIPLE OF VIBRATION

This principle states that everything is always in motion and has its own vibration. This concept is supported by theories of quantum physics. Physicists have discovered that matter is not solid, but is made up of either particles or waves that are constantly fluctuating. If you break down any object or living thing to its smallest particle, you will see that it is in motion. Even light has its own vibration. Scientist and mathematician Christian Doppler performed many experiments measuring the frequency and vibration of light.

According to this principle, every plant, tree, chair, table, and color has its own specific motion or vibration. Taking this one step further, every thought, action, and experience emits an energy and has a vibration as well. When you are able to sense an argument has taken place in a room, you are tuning in to that vibration. As discussed earlier, many of your experiences take place on an energetic or vibrational level. You produce vibrations or brain waves that can be measured with the EEG machine found in all hospitals. Even when you are in a relaxed, meditative state, you produce brain waves. The brain wave produced during this state is sometimes called "alpha." It is common among regular meditators to say they are "going into alpha."

Just as you create brain waves when you are in a relaxed, peaceful state, you also create them to help the subconscious mind re-create and seek out patterns. You are now aware that people tend to repeat patterns of behavior. They tend to become involved in relationships that re-create the feelings they experienced as children.

An adult who was abused as a child is likely, on a subconscious level, to seek out an abusive mate. The abuse usually occurs in the same way, whether it is physical or emotional. People do not wear signs that let us know how they will behave in a relationship. Yet, we still seem to know which people will meet our subconscious requirements to play out a particular pattern. This process of attraction all takes place vibrationally. Simultaneously, we emit a vibration that others sense. And because they are also subconsciously seeking to re-create emotional experiences and behavioral patterns, they may find our particular vibrations appropriate to their particular needs. In any case, whatever a person believes to be true is, for that person, true, whether favorable or unfavorable.

Our thoughts continually create a vibration that attracts people, opportunities, and experiences. Therefore, the energy we put out directly affects what is drawn to us. An example of this phenomenon is described in the cliché "when it rains, it pours." When we are in a relationship, we usually meet more people. When we are in a great mood, we usually attract fun people. When we wake up on the "wrong side of the bed," the day usually follows suit. Just as we can feel the vibrational output of others, they can feel ours. Our purpose then is to understand what messages we are sending out. These explain the experiences we are attracting. By understanding this process, we can alter and improve our lives.

PRINCIPLE 3: PRINCIPLE OF CAUSE AND EFFECT

This principle states that for every cause there is an effect, and for every effect, there is a cause. Sir Isaac Newton in his third law said: "Whenever one body exerts a force on another, the second body exerts a force equal in magnitude and opposite in direction on the first body; or to every action force there is an equal and opposite reaction force. For every action there is a reaction."

For example, a child runs through the living room of his house, knocks over a vase, and breaks it. There is a clear, superficial cause-and-effect scenario. The running child is the cause, and the broken vase is the effect. Without the cause there would be no effect. Without the running child, the vase would not be broken. The following example of the principle of cause and effect, directly relates to the principle of mentalism. A man is standing on his back porch looking out at his yard. He thinks, The lawn needs to be cut; I guess I'll mow the lawn. He then does it. His thought—the lawn needs to be cut—is the cause. The mowed lawn is the effect of that cause.

We combined the principle of mentalism with the principle of cause and effect. Since everything begins with a thought, we can conclude that the causes of most of our life experiences have stemmed from our own thoughts and deep-seated beliefs. This does not mean we create misfortune for ourselves on a conscious level. However, subconsciously we do create the experiences that are familiar to us and therefore comfortable. We are uneasy with the notion that somehow we are responsible for our experiences.

The responsibility associated with the Step-by-Step Method yields freedom, not blame.

In this chapter you have built a strong foundation of conceptual knowledge. You are now ready to begin using the Step-by-Step Method to make profound changes in your life. Part II of this book will take you through the actual process. The following summary of concepts will prepare you to take steps that will change your life for the better.

1. Ego: Experiences the everyday world through the five senses.
2. Conscious Mind: Makes generalizations from ego experience and teaches them to the subconscious mind. For example:
    - Trust: People will take advantage of you if you let them.
    - Relationships: There are many potential partners.
    - Money: There isn't enough money to go around.
    - Safety: The world isn't a very safe place.
    - Health: You are only as good as your genes.
    - Luck: The only kind of luck I have is bad.
3. Subconscious Mind: Seeks to validate generalizations by energetically recognizing and re-creating comfortable patterns and habits.
4. Principle of Mentalism: Everything begins with a thought.
5. Principle of Vibration: Everything is in constant motion.
6. Principle of Cause and Effect: For every effect there is a cause. For every cause there is an effect.

With these basic concepts in mind, you are ready to begin the journey to greater happiness, prosperity, peace of mind, and success, step by step.

Part II

THE JOURNEY

3

THE QUALITY OF YOUR QUESTIONS IMPACTS ON THE QUALITY OF YOUR LIFE

Our minds operate very much like computers. A computer solves equations using data that was input. Our minds also solve problems and answer questions. The quality of the solution we receive from a computer is only as good as the quality of the data that was entered. In the same way, the quality of the solutions or answers we receive from our minds depends on the quality of the questions we ask.

One major difference between our minds and computers is the way we process information. A computer spits out a written answer. Our minds use the power of the subconscious to seek out life experiences that show us the answer.

Problems arise when you ask yourself questions to which you do not necessarily want the answers. In a depressed state, you may ask yourself: Why can't I earn more money? Why can't I find the right relationship? Why am I so overweight? Why can't I find the right job? Why do I have all the bad luck? Why can't I stay motivated? Why am I always sick?

Our minds show us the answers, both intellectually and through life experiences. We saw in the previous chapter, that gathering more negative experiences strengthens our beliefs as to what we can or cannot have, who we can or cannot be. With this reinforced "knowledge," it becomes even more difficult to ask the right questions. We do not really want to know "why we can't." We want to know "how we can."

Scientific research shows that we access less than ten percent of our brain power. One of the goals of the Step-by-Step Method is to teach you to understand that and to access as much of it as possible. It is clear that knowledge is gained in ways that the five senses cannot always explain. Life patterns are repeated without apparent conscious effort. It is time to take control. You have used powerful methods to produce unfavorable results in your life. Now you will use those very same methods—this time to your advantage!

The following exercise will take approximately fifteen minutes. It will help make you aware of the messages you send to your subconscious through the questions you ask yourself.

EXERCISE: WHAT WENT IN IS NOW COMING OUT.

List several personal questions you ask yourself which are to your detriment. Use the examples of questions you might ask if in a depressed state. List any answers you received to the negative questions. Sometimes the answers come to mind immediately in words, but in most cases they come to us in terms of life experience, through conversations, or during the course of our lives. This means that you must be aware. You must find the meaning in events.

Now that you are aware that the questions you ask yourself affect your experience and beliefs, you have a powerful tool. It is time to use the same techniques to ask purposeful, positive questions. The rest of this chapter focuses on ways to improve the quality of your questions.

In posing questions, one of the most important things to remember is to phrase them positively. There are many ways to ask a question that may appear to be positive but are not. For example: "How can I stop being lazy? How can I get rid of this lousy attitude? How can I stop attracting bad relationships?" These are all negative questions. They state that the person asking the question owns the negative qualities they want to be rid of, that they are themselves negative. This is negative programming or reinforcing. You need to imply that you own the positive qualities you are striving to achieve, that you are yourself positive.

Why not try: "How can I increase my motivation? How can I improve my attitude? How can I attract the correct relationship for me?" The difference may be subtle to the ego or personality, but it effects the subconscious mind at a deep level. This shift in language programs the mind to seek out and experience positive outcomes.

Compared to the resourcefulness of the subconscious, the ego is quite limited. The subconscious filters through myriad stimuli to find an energy that is familiar and simultaneously radiates energy to attract. The ego gathers information only through the five senses. Because the ego has limited access to information, it assumes that options are limited. However, the ego is only the personality, and you are much more than that. Many of us feel our options are limited because we have in the past experienced limitation. We believe that we must find answers to all life's challenges on the basis of our intellect or the superficial level of the ego. In reality, this is not so.

Have you ever been working on a problem the solution to which seems out of reach? Finally fed up, you decide to go for a walk, get a snack, or take a nap. After resting, a solution suddenly comes to you. This is not the work of the ego. The ego could not find the answer. It is the work of the subconscious. The ego gave the subconscious pieces of a puzzle. When the ego relaxed, the deeper and more sensitive subconscious was able to go to work and come up with an answer.

The subconscious mind operates on an energetic level, accessing people, events, opportunities, and answers on a similar energetic frequency. Carl Jung referred to this energetic bank as the collective unconscious. The subconscious mind, in its full capacity, is the great orchestrator of events as it invisibly seeks out and repels circumstances so that our lives mirror our beliefs. The ego doesn't have to know how this takes place—only that it does.

Our minds find wonderful answers when we ask the right questions. These questions are the causes that generate effects. This concept brings you to the next exercise which will help you to use these theories for practical purposes. Your new questions will provoke improvements in your life. The following exercise will take approximately thirty minutes.

EXERCISE: PART I. GET READY FOR A CHANGE.

Make a list of categories that you consider significant to your life. For example:

1. *Relationships*
2. *Health*
3. *Career*
4. *Money*
5. *Spirituality*
6. *Fears*

Under each heading think of at least one question that, when answered, would provide you with clarity and updated information. The following are examples of categories and questions. You will create questions that are meaningful to you.

Examples:

1. *Relationships*
    What can I do to get along well with my mother?
    What can I do to attract a new relationship?
    How can I maintain harmony between myself and ______?
    How can I renew my passion for my wife/husband?
2. *Health*
    What can I do to achieve perfect health?
    How can I eat to achieve my ideal weight?
    How can I motivate myself to exercise?
    How can I increase my energy level?

3. Career

How can I effectively position myself for a promotion?
What can I do to improve my work performance?
How can I renew my passion for work?
What can I do to find the perfect job for me?
How can I find work that inspires me?
What should I do with my career?
What can I do to find work that utilizes my skills?

4. Money

What can I do to increase my income by twenty percent?
What can I do to attract more customers?
How can I find the best money manager for me?

5. Spirituality

What can I do to align myself with my highest purpose?
How can I attain inner peace?
How can I show unconditional love for myself and others?

6. Fears

How can I speak publicly with ease and eloquence?
How can I remain calm throughout my day?
How can I interact with my family in a healthy way?
How can I live worry free?

The following exercise takes less than thirty seconds a day. This is the practical application of question-asking.

EXERCISE: PART II. EXPERIENCE THE CHANGE.

Pick one question from the list you made during the first part of the exercise. Start with the question that evokes the most passion for you. Each morning, as soon as you wake up, ask yourself the question with passion and energy. Know that your mind will *find the answer for you, just as it found the answers to the negative questions you have been asking all your life.*

Ask one question at a time for a two-week period. In the evening, or once or twice during the day, write the question down when it comes to mind. This will add reinforcement. There is no need to be obsessive. When you ask with passion and a real desire for the answer, you will receive it. Our tendency is to push the elevator button over and over even when we know that pushing it does not make the elevator come any faster. The answer will come. It always does. Your job is to listen.

I recommend doing this exercise first thing in the morning. There are two main reasons for this recommendation. The first is a common phenomenon to those who wake up to the radio. When the alarm goes off, the first song you hear in the morning plays over and over in your mind for the entire day. You do not have to make this happen; it happens whether you want it to or not. This exercise allows you to use this phenomenon to your benefit. Let your mind play your question over and over again until it finds the answer.

The second reason for practicing this exercise first thing in the morning is that your mind is then not yet cluttered with the day's activities. Furthermore, when you first wake up there will be less interference from the ego.

Answers come in many forms. They may be in the form of an insight from a friend. They may come to you while you are in the shower. One may just pop into your mind when you are eating a snack, or it might appear as an opportunity. You never know when or how the answer will come.

Keep track of the information that comes to you. Keeping a record is important. In the future, you may resist using the exercise to tackle other areas in your life. This record will help break down the resistance as it verifies the power and effectiveness of this simple step.

In this chapter you have learned the following:

1. Your mind is like a computer. It solves problems and finds answers to questions asked.
2. The quality of the questions you ask yourself, either positive or negative, relates directly to the quality of the answers you receive.
3. The ego or personality believes that options are limited because it can only gather information through the five senses. The sub-

conscious mind is unlimited because it accesses information energetically, beyond the reach of the five senses.

4. Using the subconscious mind to seek out solutions gives you unlimited potential for solutions and answers, well beyond that of the intellect or ego.

In this chapter you have also taken the first step in making profound changes in your life in the following ways:

1. You have acknowledged that you may have negatively programmed your subconscious mind by asking negative questions.
2. You have refocused the old questions, making them positive in order to receive positive information.
3. You have changed one area of your behavior that may have contributed to negative or limiting programming.
4. You have accessed a powerful internal resource that you can use at any time.

In the next chapter, we will go one step further, and begin tackling and harnessing the power and nature of habits. We will alter existing habits and form new habits that will help rather than hinder your personal growth.

4

SIX HABITS TO CHANGE

In Chapter 3 you made one simple improvement in your life. You changed the way you ask yourself questions. Instead of using negative programming, you switched to positive programming. The way you phrase questions is a result of your personal speech pattern, a habit you have developed over the years. Your speech habit may be so ingrained you are unaware of the particular dialect or sort of phrasing you use. However, even speech habits can be changed. One of the permanent life improvements the Step-by-Step Method fosters is not only awareness of, but the ability to change unproductive or unhealthy habits. This chapter focuses on how you can replace old habits with those that generate success and happiness.

You have already changed one small habit. Now you are ready to change larger ones. This step is crucial because your life is made up of habits. Everything you do is out of habit. You can attribute how you dress, how you respond to conversation, and even how you think to habit. Most of your habits have been with you for a major part of your life and are constantly being reinforced. You are now going to reprogram your habits to produce the kind of results you want.

There are six major habits that must be altered in order to prepare yourself for living a fully abundant life. Even if you proceed no further, once having modified these habits, you will see your world begin to change. Recalling the principle of cause and effect, altering these habits will change the cause of the unsatisfactory effects in your life.

The six habits that you will be working on are:

1. Blocking the flow
2. Crowding
3. Limited beliefs
4. Fear
5. Self-sabotage/limited comfort zone
6. Lack of gratitude

BLOCKING THE FLOW

It is important to remember that everything is in motion. The natural course of events, or the "flow," consists of our being able subconsciously to seek out experiences to fulfill our desires or beliefs. Blocking the flow represents the artificial halting of the process of seeking out information or experiences energetically.

At some point in our lives we have learned to hold tightly to what we want. We all feel a great sense of control this way. We are under the illusion that we can actually keep what we want by controlling it. It is time to break that habit.

When you grab hold of what you want and squeeze too tightly, you stop your output of energy that attracts people, situations, and opportunities to you. You block the flow. In most cases blocking the flow stems from fear of losing whatever it is you are trying to control. Ironically, blocking the flow often creates what you fear most, which is losing what you are holding on to. Creating the flow offers opportunities to give you what you want. This concept of creating or blocking the flow of energy is complex, and best explained through a case study.

Emily K.: Emily is a mother of two children, now in their twenties. Her main concern was a deteriorating relationship with her children. She felt that her children spent time with her out of guilt, rather than love. She was resentful when her children made time for other people, yet disappointed when they made time for her because it felt obligatory.

Emily needed to be reminded that people receive information energetically. It was possible that her children were sensing her disappointment. We talked about the possibility that she was actually pushing her children away by clutching and controlling them.

Over time, the situation escalated. I suggested that she try to create an emotional space for her children that would give them room to come and go so they could spend time with her of their own volition. I cautioned her that her behavior changes needed to include controlling her impulse to "guilt trip" them when they were busy.

Emily was nervous about letting go of the nagging behavior because she felt she would never see her children. However, realizing she had no choice, she tried the new approach. Emily called one of her daughters, and told her that she would love to get together with her when her daughter was available. In keeping with their established pattern, her daughter became defensive, and said that she was busy. Instead of Emily's usual response—"You are always too busy"—she said, "I understand. When you are free and are up to a visit, give me a call. I'd love to see you." Emily let her daughter know that she wanted to see her, but this time she allowed her daughter room in which to maneuver. Emily delivered no innuendos and made no accusations or attempts to control her daughter's response.

> Several days later Emily's daughter called her back and made plans to visit. Their next few visits remained somewhat tense, but Emily continued to practice her new behavior. It took approximately six months for Emily to attain the kind of relationship with her daughters that she had always wanted. She realized that by giving them the freedom and approval to do what they needed to do for themselves, she actually had created a comfortable space for all of them. Her behavior showed them that she had unconditional love for them. She now gave her daughters what she wanted for herself—unforced love, comfortable interactions, and joy in just being together.

There are literally hundreds of examples of people squeezing what they want rather than creating a flow around it. Creating the flow is the act of letting go of panic and giving first, rather than holding, controlling, or demanding that what you want for yourself, come to you. For Emily, giving first meant offering her daughters unforced love.

We have all watched the behavior of people who feel insecure about a relationship. The first thing they do is make demands, act jealous, and create a general heaviness in the relationship. This type of behavior actually creates what they fear most. The pursued person feels the weight of the demands and begins to pull away. Because experiences are perceived energetically, the clinging partner senses the imminent loss and holds on even tighter. This snowball effect destroys many relationships.

This process of blocking the flow occurs in all areas of life including career, relationships, financial matters, etc. In order to stop blocking the flow and to start creating it, you must *first* stop clutching at whatever it is that you want, and start demonstrating a relaxed posture through actions and attitude. Managed motion changes emotion, and creates a new cause for a new effect. Your new, confident behavior will be crucial in convincing the subconscious mind that your situation has changed. By adopting a more casual attitude you are telling your subconscious mind that there is plenty there for you. On the other hand, when you cling to something out of fear, you tell your subconscious that there is not enough.

Take money, for instance. Many people have financial concerns. As money is merely a form of energy exchange, it can represent many things, such as security, comfort, or independence. If you want more money, you must first discover what it means to you. Once you know what it means to you, demonstrate your confidence in this area. It may be that you are in a position to give money to the needy. If you are able to, do it. The idea of creating the flow is to avoid the overanxious waiting for checks to roll in. Do not grab in fear and panic. Relinquish your hold and relax.

Dare to break the habit of blocking the flow. Although you may not experience in an instant what you are looking for, by creating the flow, you can create the energy that attracts it. As your perception changes, so does your world. It is not easy to attract love when you are removed from it. As you create the flow, you reteach your subconscious mind not only that what you are looking for is available to you, but that you are ready and comfortable with having it.

Your subconscious mind will then create the experience, and it will allow it into your life. You ready yourself for the experience by already being in it. You are acting with faith and trust that what you want is accessible to you. It is a statement of fearlessness. Make a conscious effort to create the flow in your everyday life.

The following exercise will take approximately twenty minutes to complete.

EXERCISE: ME FIRST!

Think of something you would like to have in your life right now, such as peace of mind, a new relationship, more money, a better job, more leisure time.

On a piece of paper, list all the ways you can think of, no matter how farfetched, to create the flow of energy necessary to attain what you want. When doing this, it is important to remember what your wish means to YOU. (Money = comfort, love = security).

There are many ways to create the flow of similar energies. Here are just a few examples of how to create the flow of money, if money means independence to you:

- *If someone is lost, take time and give them great directions.*
- *Assist a friend in finding an apartment.*
- *Help someone with his/her resume.*
- *Let out-of-town friends stay with you.*

If money means comfort:

- *Have people over for dinner.*
- *Visit a sick relative and bring along soup.*
- *Offer assistance to a friend.*
- *Clean up your house.*

You can always create a flow of energy. By giving first, you immediately feel rich in that area, and you create the energy that allows you to receive. Like energies attract. When it rains, it pours.

If it is love that you want, you can create the flow by:

- *Listening compassionately to a friend who has a problem.*
- *Allowing someone the freedom to be themselves.*
- *Offering a homeless person a sandwich.*
- *Giving loved ones the room to live in your heart without feeling cramped.*

If you are looking for peace of mind, abundance, health, beauty, energy, or even creativity, find ways to create the flow. At times, creating the flow may just be an internal experience. For example: if you would like to radiate beauty, see it in others.

There are many ways to create the flow of similar energies. One of these almost magical ways is the concept of acting "as if." Emily acted as if she had no fear of losing her daughters. This acting created a flow, whereby the relationship between them strengthened. The process of acting "as if" can be accomplished if you recall a time in your life when you felt, looked, and acted in a way that you would like to re-create now. For example: When business is going well, you may stand taller, pay more attention to how you dress, socialize more with friends, feel more confident on sales calls, or act more patient with your children and spouse.

Acting "as if" allows you to neutralize the limiting belief that outside stimuli are necessary to change your mood. The acting "as if" principal works by sending messages to the subconscious which are already recognizable and which create experiences as well as feelings.

Acting "as if" is not to be confused with denial. It is conscious thought management, an effective way to change your mood, thereby your experience. Emotions create a snowball effect. When things are going well, you feel good and more things go well. When things are going poorly, you feel depressed or ineffective, and more things go poorly. Acting "as if" allows you to take charge of a situation by stopping the negative snowball before it starts. It will also make you feel better. Instead of allowing outside circumstances to dictate what happens to you, create the vibration or energy of what you want to be happening in your life. Before you know it, you will no longer be acting.

Ron R. and Paul K.: Ron and Paul are salesmen for a small software company. Business had been slow for the entire sales force for over five months. It had been especially slow for them. Ron, Paul, and two other salespeople, attended one of my motivational seminars. During the seminar they were introduced to the concept of acting "as if." To test the concept's validity, Paul and Ron were assigned the task of spending the next week acting "as if" business was great. The other two salespeople were to maintain their normal behavior.

After one week, Ron had written one contract and Paul had scheduled his second appointment with a company to make a bid for a contract. This was more activity than either had seen in months. The other two salespeople did not have any activity and immediately began acting "as if."

Take as long as you would like with this next exercise.

EXERCISE: ACTING "AS IF"

Take a moment to remember a time in your life when you felt exhilarated, successful, and loved. Enjoy the memory.

CROWDING

"Crowding" is the act of filling your life with things that are not right for you, thereby limiting your ability to reach for what you truly want. You will be changing the habit of crowding into the habit of "creating a vacuum." Creating a vacuum is the act of mentally or physically ridding yourself of things, circumstances, or relationships that no longer serve you. When you create a vacuum, you make room for something new to come into your life.

In some circumstances you may want to create the vacuum in the physical world, not just mentally. For example, it is difficult to draw someone into a new relationship when you are still emotionally and physically involved in another one. When much of your attention is focused on some other person, people sense that you are involved and unavailable, and in many cases potential partners will not be drawn to you.

Maya S.: Maya had a part-time job while she was building a private consulting practice. She knew that she needed to devote more time to her business, but was uncomfortable about leaving her part-time job for security reasons. It took Maya over a year to leave because of her fear. While she was crowding, her practice did not grow. Not only did she have less time because of the hours she spent at the part-time job, but she was often drained and did not have the energy to effectively utilize the little time she had.

After Maya left the part-time job, she felt more like an entrepreneur and adopted that stance. Apparently out of nowhere, opportunities arose and filled her time with work that supported her financially. Had Maya not left the job, she would have continued to feel as though she were unable to support herself in her chosen profession and these profitable opportunities would have passed her by!

Erica A.: Erica would look in her closet every day and feel annoyed at how few of her outfits she actually wore. Several friends suggested that she make room in the overstuffed space for new clothes by giving away the old ones. For months she refused to let go of what she did not need. However, when spring arrived, Erica decided to do some cleaning. She gave away everything she no longer wanted. Her closet looked bare, but over the next few months, whenever there was a sale Erica went shopping. She very slowly added new articles of clothing to her wardrobe. It was easy for her to see what she really needed, and now she was happy with everything she owned. The big surprise came on her birthday, when all of the presents she received were clothing. Her friends and family had noticed her empty closet and had decided to help her fill it up.

Creating a vacuum or ending crowding need not always take place in the physical world. If you have a job that is not right for you, you do not necessarily have to quit it and cut off your income. You must, however, at least mentally dissociate yourself from your workplace. Dissociating yourself means that you no longer become involved in office politics and no longer get caught up in the injustices or dramas at work. In this way your job will take up less space in your life and you will be creating a vacuum.

> **Alexander H.:** Alex was unhappy with his work. He did not like his boss or the way his department was managed. He talked for an hour about his frustration. He felt trapped in his position because financially he could not afford to leave until he found another. He unintentionally expressed his anger and frustration during job interviews, which made it difficult to make a good impression on prospective employers.
>
> Alex's first task was to list the aspects of his job that he did not like. Then he set out to mentally dissociate himself from those aspects, and to focus on his job and anything that he enjoyed at work. At first this was difficult. After two weeks it was easier to avoid conversations that drew him into office complaining sessions. Without reinforcing the negative side every day, he started feeling better about work. He concentrated on performing the aspects of his job that he liked and his attitude improved immensely. His job interviews went better. Within two months of dissociating himself from the office environment, Alex found a new job.

Crowding radiates doubt and fear. If you knew that when you ended a harmful relationship, a new and more satisfying one would take its place, would you end it? You probably would. When you create a vacuum you are retraining your subconscious and giving it the message that there are more opportunities, that you deserve better. Armed with this information, the subconscious begins to seek out something new.

Letting go of outmoded aspects of your life is difficult. You feel resistant to it for many reasons. You fear the loss of a sense of security, and experience a fear of the unknown. However, even with these difficulties, there are ways to create a vacuum that will produce satisfying results, both physically and mentally.

The next exercise is a practice run for ridding ourselves of the crowded aspects of our lives. The written part will take approximately five minutes. The time frame for carrying out the exercise is individual. You decide when you would like to have it completed.

EXERCISE: THIS HAS GOT TO GO!

Make a list of at least five things you own that you no longer need or want.

Examples:

- *Old clothes*
- *Dishes*
- *Books*
- *Stuffed animals*
- *Old high school papers*
- *Brown paper bags in your kitchen*

Imagine how good it will feel to have clean closets or a clean desk. Just think how good it will feel to clean out your life. Now remove them from your life in any way that is appropriate: selling, giving away, or recycling.

LIMITED BELIEFS

Your belief system consists of your personal set of generalizations or "truths." They are learned beliefs (about relationships, security, peace of mind, happiness, etc.) that have been repeatedly reinforced over the years. Changing your belief system is difficult to do because, with the help of your subconscious mind, you have become skilled at collecting evidence to support those beliefs. To create a new belief system in any area of your life, you must allow yourself faith and patience while you attract new experiences that validate a new way of thinking.

Many thought processes can be limiting. Some of the most common of these are:

- There isn't enough love, money, opportunity, etc. to go around.
- I can't have all the money I need.
- I am not attractive.

- I could never be in a perfect relationship; there aren't enough good men/women in this town.
- The perfect career or job does not exist.
- I have to settle for less than I really want.
- Real happiness is a fairy tale.
- Spiritual people don't earn a lot of money.

If any of these restrictive beliefs are yours, it is safe to say that you have had experiences that supported them. However, now is the time to tackle your beliefs and make them work for you instead of against you.

Because beliefs are built and reinforced over time, it is unrealistic to expect that you can change them overnight. So, instead of changing your thoughts, you need to develop a new habit that will change your experience. This will build a foundation for new beliefs.

Improving on old ways of thinking requires behavior modification. As discussed earlier, everything begins with a thought. It is unrealistic to expect yourself to wipe out unfavorable thoughts instantly. What you *can* immediately change is your speech.

By changing your speech patterns you immediately change the vibration of your thoughts. For example: If someone asks how your business is, instead of saying, "Business is awful," try, "It hasn't been as good as I would like, but I'm looking forward to it turning around." If someone asks you why you are not married yet, instead of explaining that it's hard to meet people and all the good ones are taken, you may want to say, "I'm open to meeting someone. It just hasn't happened yet."

Changing your words slowly and surely changes your attitude. Attitudes carry their own vibrations just as thoughts do. They draw people to you or repel them. All opportunities come through people, and we are most drawn to people with bright outlooks and visions for the future. Why limit your opportunities when, by simply changing your habit of speech, you can draw more people to you and create a new horizon? As your attitude improves, your vibrational output will also improve, as will your internal beliefs, and you will feel better about yourself and your life. Improving attitudes through the power of expression is a catalyst for wondrous results.

> **John R.:** John had a hard time motivating himself in the morning. He wanted to find a quick, noncaffeinated way to get energized and ready to start the day. In combing through the details of his morning routine, it turned out that he often ritually complained of having to wake up and go to work. This behavior was more of a habit than anything else, as he actually liked his job.
>
> He combined the question-asking technique with the attitude-improvement theory and found the charge he needed in the morning. Now every day when he wakes up he says, "What a great day for an adventure!" He no longer has problems getting up and out of bed. He energetically gears himself up for a great day.

Beliefs are so powerful that they create or limit what you experience. In fact, many experiments have been conducted to measure just how powerful beliefs can be. The most noted of these measured the effectiveness of placebo medication for pain patients. In World War II, the use of placebos was common and frequently effective in treating the pain of wounded soldiers when morphine and other pain medication was scarce.

No matter how powerful your beliefs, your words have power to change them, as do your actions. If you stood in the middle of your living room and repeated over and over again "I'm never going to have enough money," you would begin to feel anxious and depressed. If you did it long enough, you would develop a deep belief that you really were not going to have enough. With this belief you'd be sure to miss opportunities to fulfill your needs.

On the other hand, if you stand in the middle of your living room and repeat "Opportunities to make money flow into my life," you will feel elated when you are done and will see opportunities all around you. This exercise is an exaggerated example of what you do every day of your life.

One of the most powerful things I have done for myself in my transition from being a commercial mortgage financier to a teacher and writer was to call myself just that: a teacher and writer. At first it felt uncomfortable. However, as I began to use those words in describing my work, I began to say them, to feel them, and to believe them. My new feelings allowed me to live my life in that capacity.

The following exercise has five parts. The written part of it, which is designed to help you identify any limiting beliefs you may have, should take approximately sixty minutes.

EXERCISE: TIME TO TELL IT LIKE IT IS

List any phrases or statements you regularly make that may undermine your success or happiness. For example: "I'll never make enough money," or "I'll never find the right partner."

Now, write a brief narrative of what your life would look like if you changed those beliefs. How would you rephrase those statements to reflect a more positive outlook?

After the narrative, assess whether or not it would be worth changing your belief systems (now that you know how powerful and limiting they can be).

If you decide that it would be worth changing your beliefs to allow yourself to live the way you described in your narration, write down how you would act if you were living as you described.

Now, act "as if." Enjoy it, live it, and allow it to come to fruition.

The next habit to discuss, is the habit that can stay with us for a lifetime unless we dedicate ourselves to changing it. That habit is fear.

FEAR

Fear is one response to the unknown. When you face the unknown you have a built-in defense mechanism that wants to protect you. Although the unknown can be a positive thing, it can still create fear. Many people experience fear before starting a new job, even if it is the job of their dreams. Change can evoke fear. Therefore, fear is something you experience at various times as your life shifts and improves. Even success can feel foreign and create fear.

Fear is what keeps people in abusive relationships. If your belief system teaches you that relationships are dangerous, it may feel less dangerous to be familiar with the type of harm you are experiencing, rather than to face something unknown.

Fear is not always a bad thing. It acts as a warning, and makes you take things slowly. There are many categories of fears: fear of abandonment, fear of failure, fear of loneliness, or fear of poverty, just to name a few. Problems arise when you let the fear of the unknown stop you from reaching for a better life. In order to reach your goals of a better life, you need to break the habit of letting fear stop you.

Acknowledge your fears, call them by name, and assess the next appropriate step to release the fears that impede your progress. The following is an example of doing just that.

> **Teddy A.:** Teddy's parents groomed him educationally and emotionally to be a doctor. The entire family took pride in the fact that Teddy was going to be the first doctor in the family. This career was picked for him when we was just a child. The family tells the story of how his mother would hold baby Teddy and say, "He has the hands of a surgeon."
>
> As expected, before graduating from Harvard Teddy began applying to medical school. As he was, he began to think of all of the other things he might like to do with his life. He casually mentioned to his parents that he felt a passion for environmental protection and that he might be interested in pursuing a career in that field. The notion was dismissed. Teddy was accepted at a medical school and went.
>
> He was not happy there and wanted to take a leave of absence. The family was upset by this and told him he

was being ridiculous. Of course he wanted to be a doctor, he had always wanted to be a doctor. Teddy grew more and more anxious and unhappy and began to do poorly in his studies. His friends told him to just leave school and pursue the career he wanted. He felt that he could not, that he must stay in school. When people asked him why, at first he was not sure.

Teddy placed himself under pressure to make a decision. He decided to finish school and become a doctor, and he did just that.

He still was not happy. His family was. Seven years passed and Teddy was in his mid-thirties, practicing medicine. At this point he decided to face the fears he had and to make a decision about his future.

Teddy determined that he had been afraid to leave medical school for a variety of reasons: He would feel like a failure; he would feel that he had failed his parents; he had never seriously thought of himself as anything but a doctor, and he did not know who he would be if he was not a physician. He feared if he chose another career and then failed he could not live with himself. These fears had kept him in medical school and then working at a job that made him unhappy.

He finally named his fears. In doing so, they became less frightening and he was able to face them. Teddy slowly worked through his fears by talking about them and putting alternatives into perspective. He determined the price he would have to pay if he pursued his dreams. Stress, the disappointment of those who wished to control him, facing the unknown, and risking failure. Once he determined the price he would have to pay, he made an agreement with himself to pay it. It was not easy for him, but he left medicine and returned to school to prepare for a career in environmental safety, his true passion. Teddy is now happy with his career.

It took several years for his parents to work through their disappointment. Eventually, though, they saw that their son was happy and came to terms with Teddy's choice.

Fear can be found in many circumstances. The following exercise will assist you in facing your fears. It should take approximately twenty minutes.

EXERCISE:MONSTERS IN THE CLOSET

Name one area of your life where you suspect fear has interfered. (Not trying out for sports, not asking someone out on a date, changing careers, pursuing a study in music or art, etc.) Name the fear.

Is there a price that would have to be paid to work through this fear? What price? Determine if it is worth it. If it is, find resources to support you and resolve to pay the price. If paying the price is not worth it, find a way to make peace around the awareness.

SELF-SABOTAGE/LIMITED COMFORT ZONE

As you work through fear there is bound to be resistance. You may discover such resistance when bumping into the wall of your comfort zone. A comfort zone is an artificial, self-imposed barrier that your subconscious mind creates that allows you to feel or know when you are approaching the limit of what you believe you can experience or have. For example: if Mary has never been treated with respect in a relationship, and begins dating a caring, loving person, this relationship exceeds her comfort zone, causing either anxiety or fear or a subconscious desire to run or destroy the relationship. When you approach the limit of your comfort zone, it creates a feeling of uneasiness or impending doom. Self-sabotage usually occurs in response to the feeling that the situation is too good to be true. You unconsciously want your life to reflect your beliefs. If your life begins to exceed your beliefs, you tend to find a way to adjust your beliefs or to adjust your experience.

Self-sabotage is often the response to an experience that surpasses your current belief systems. If something is too good, too much, or too fast, you subconsciously find a way to bring it back to a level that is comfortable, in line with what you believe you can have.

Self-sabotage can be subtle. You may be in danger of sabotaging your success if you continually find yourself thinking or saying, "Just when I thought everything was going so well . . ." or if you take pride in all of the mishaps in your life. You may be a self-sabotager if you energetically relay your tales of woe to friends. In a much more subtle way, self-sabotage may be imminent if you feel anxious when pieces of your life are falling into place. Having daydreams about catching your partner being unfaithful may be indicative of self-sabotage. These are a few signs of being at the limit of, or of having exceeded, a belief system.

Our success sometimes exceeds our highest expectations. This reality confronts the artificial limitation of our beliefs. In this way it forces you to look at the way you create your life experience. If you sabotage a pattern of success, this enables you to say, "See, I knew it was too good to be true." This pattern alleviates the burden of trying for more.

To move past self-sabotage, you must first recognize it. If you realize that you have reached the limits of your beliefs, you may use the power of words to gently push these limits. Feel yourself becoming comfortable with a greater field of success. Find a sentence that you can repeat to yourself to help you move to the next level. Example of phrases to use:

- I easily and naturally give and receive love.
- My past is my past. I am ready for a wonderful future.
- I expand my range of experiences with ease.
- I allow more into my life.
- I comfortably allow abundance into my life.
- I am comfortable making more money.

David L.: David is a department manager for a national accounting firm. Until last year, he was one of thirty accountants in the department. David's manager was retiring and he recommended that David replace him.

Suddenly, David was the boss. He found himself in a position of responsibility for which he was not emotionally prepared. He was both competent and skilled enough to do a good job. However, the position exceeded his comfort level of success, and he began making mistakes.

To expand his comfort zone, David went through a process of identifying why he was anxious about his new job. Although intellectually he knew that he was qualified, emotionally he feared that he would fail and be demoted. He felt like an impostor in the new position. These emotions began to allow his fear to become reality by distracting him so that he made careless mistakes.

David used positive phrases to recondition his subconscious to allow success at his job. He repeated to himself, "I am capable, qualified, and calm in performing my new job." Each time he proved to himself that he was an effective manager, it further served to expand his level of comfort in his position. Although he works constantly on the feelings surrounding success and his career, David no longer exhibits self-sabotaging behaviors.

The following exercise will help to identify the times in your past when an experience exceeded your comfort zone. This should take approximately fifteen minutes.

EXERCISE:DID I DO THAT TO ME?

List any time within the past year that a positive experience made you feel uncomfortable. What belief did that experience challenge the truth of? How did you handle the discomfort. Be scrupulously honest with yourself in answering. Did you sabotage the experience?

Write either "yes" or "no" to the following question. Are you ready to make a change? If you answered no, that is fine. Come back to the exercise when the answer is yes. We all have our own time frames. If the answer is yes, find a way to make a change by retraining your subconscious mind.

LACK OF GRATITUDE

Being grateful slowly eases fear and anger by aligning yourself with love. It also subtly changes your subconscious focus from "not enough" to appreciation. If someone gives you a gift that is not exactly what you wanted, and you are annoyed, you will be unable to enjoy the gift. It will also be less likely that you will be receiving another gift from that person. Gratefully accepting what you have in your life while you are working on making improvements, subconsciously aligns you to receive more, as well as allows you to enjoy what you already have.

Feeling grateful creates a flow, loosens energy blocks in your body, puts out love energy, and creates a beautiful energy around you that attracts people and opportunity. Being truly grateful allows you to enjoy the gifts you receive by being alive. We have more to be grateful for than we usually acknowledge.

Take as much time as you would like with the following exercise. It is designed to put you in touch with the many wonderful things you have in your life. This is a good exercise to do daily.

EXERCISE: EXPERIENCING GRATITUDE

Make a list of everything you can be grateful for.

Examples:

- *Good friends*
- *Shelter*
- *Food*
- *Good health*
- *Children*
- *Parents*
- *Pets*
- *Sense of style*
- *Spirituality and guidance*

- *Growth*
- *Partner/mate/spouse*
- *Career*
- *Freedom*
- *Sense of humor*

Feeling appreciation for what you already have in your life allows greater enjoyment of life itself. Being grateful subconsciously aligns you with the positive in every experience, rather than the negative. The experience may not immediately change but your perception will.

It takes a tremendous amount of courage to face the difficult habits, beliefs and fears discussed in this chapter. By doing so, you made a commitment to having more success, love, and joy in your life. You are taking charge and creating a new future for yourself.

In this chapter you learned to identify six habits and how to change them:

1. Blocking the Flow: clutching on to what you want
    a) Letting go and giving first subconsciously aligns you to receive.
    b) Acting "as if" interferes with the habit of allowing yourself to be swept along by outside events.
2. Crowding: filling your life with things that you do not want in fear that there will be nothing to replace them
    a) Create a vacuum by either physically or emotionally making room in your life for what you do want.
3. Limited Beliefs: limiting your experiences because of what your subconscious believes you can have
    a) Retrain your subconscious through your use of language and behavior modification.
4. Fear: your response to the unknown
    a) Identify the fear.
    b) Decide the price you will have to pay to alleviate it.
    c) Determine if the price is worth it to you.
    d) If it is, pay it.

5. Self-sabotage: A subconscious response when you approach the artificial barrier, to your comfort zone
    a) Retrain your subconscious to allow greater experiences in your life.
6. Gratitude: the act of appreciation for what is already in your life
    a) Being grateful subconsciously aligns you with receiving.

You have created a strong foundation for change and are on the way to being able to embrace wonderful new experiences and successes. The next chapters are filled with Step-by-Step Methods designed to help you create your dreams so that you can fill your life with all that you can imagine.

5

DARING TO DREAM

Two years ago, during a conversation with my mother, I was describing the general work I was doing and a lecture I was about to give. Before she responded there was a long pause in the conversation. She then said, "What made you think you could do all that?" She did not ask the question because she thought I had a lot of nerve to think I was good enough to teach. Her intent was to determine how I had come to have the life I was describing to her. How had it happened? What made me try? She was genuinely curious. She could not understand why I had given up a successful career in finance to do something completely different, or why the idea had even entered my mind.

I considered my mother's question for a long time. My answer began with how unfulfilled and unhappy I had felt. I thought back to when, while still working in the financial field, I had just begun to enjoy the results of concepts that make up the Step-by-Step Method, and was learning firsthand how powerful and miraculous they could be. I had begun to believe, on a deep level, that there was more to life than I had envisioned previously, and that I did not have to settle for less than I really wanted.

During that period, I began to allow myself to dream about how my ideal life would look. I thought about it and spent time creating visual images of it in such detail that I began to feel both excited and nervous about the arrival of my new life. I was resistant to many of the details I had envisioned because they seemed out of reach. However, using the tools you have just learned, I allowed myself to face my fears, and asked myself some frightening questions.

What happens if I continue to live the way I am living?
What happens if I reach for my dreams?
What do I have to give up to do this?
What price will I have to pay?
Can I pay the price?
What if I fail?
What will become of me if I can't reach my dreams?
What if I succeed?

Although these questions were frightening, in the end I decided to do what is called "Leaping into the Void." Leaping into the Void is the process of giving up something you know for something you do not know. This process requires a decision to have faith, or to temporarily suspend disbelief in having something new.

I left a career in finance to become a teacher and writer. I have since realized that the fear of leaping is usually worse than the actual jump. It took over a year for me to completely leave my old career because I was still accustomed to focusing on why change was impossible. However, slowly but surely, I let go of all ties to an unsatisfying but secure career, and filled in my time with more teaching and writing.

Changes like this start with the Law of Mentalism described in Part I of this book. This is the simple theory that everything begins with a thought. We take the new thought about our lives, and create new vibrations through dreaming and seeing in our minds the vivid details of how we would like our perfect lives to be. Details allow us to become passionate about the picture. This passion is the trigger or "cause" for the subconscious seeking out the experiences that fit the new exciting picture or "effect."

This process can be illustrated in the following way. Search for the largest tree you can find. It did not just appear. That large tree grew from a tiny seed. Our lives are very much like that tree. Our thoughts are like the decision to plant the tree. Our dreams provide the impetus for putting the seed in the soil. Our passion nourishes the seed, and sets our dreams in motion.

This is not about idle daydreaming or fantasizing about winning the lottery. This is about a thought that moves you beyond your current belief system, expands your current comfort zone, and pushes you beyond where you think you can be. Dreaming passionately allows you to aspire to be something more than you are right now.

I am more fulfilled in my work today, because I allowed myself to dream. I decided to accept the initial discomfort of stretching my beliefs. I stopped listening to outside advice based on other people's fear and began to follow my heart.

People attending prosperity workshops typically find their limiting self-concepts challenged. When asked how much they would like to earn, the echoed response is striking. "I'd like to make $60,000 a year. No wait, that's too much, maybe $50,000, no $40,000, okay $35,000. Yeah, $35,000 is good but I'd be happy with a steady $30,000." The rest of the group nods in agreement. Sound familiar?

This person would like to earn $60,000. He believes this is impossible. Thinking about the possibility makes him uncomfortable. Therefore, he revises his desire to fit his belief, and seeks experiences to back up that belief. He will never earn more than $30,000 even though he wants to earn $60,000. Why? Subconsciously his beliefs limit his income by binding him to corresponding opportunities. Certain that he can only be paid a limited amount, he gathers evidence to back up the notion that $60,000 is completely out of reach. This continuous loop of belief-creating behavior and reinforcing belief is difficult to end.

In order to get off this treadmill, you must engage your creativity and dream about opportunities that may seem impossible.

Allow yourself to dream that you can take dramatic steps and live courageously. Let your dreams be outrageous and fanciful. Fill in all the details. When you release the beliefs that bind you, many of your dreams will begin to take form.

Dreaming techniques assist you in changing your belief system and the subsequent responses that have served as a barrier to your perfect life. These techniques will enable you to draw whatever it is you need into your life easily and sometimes miraculously.

Is there something easily identifiable in your life that you would like to have? Lower weight? Higher energy? Better health? Whatever it is, identify it and do the following exercise. The exercise will take approximately fifteen minutes.

EXERCISE: TO DREAM IT, IS TO BE IT.

Make a list of some of the things you would like to be, have, or do. For example: more money or a good relationship. Choose one of them. Find a comfortable place to sit or lie down, where you will not be disturbed. Close your eyes. Take three or more very slow, deep breaths and feel yourself relaxing. Visualize, or feel yourself already having the desired experience. For example, if you want more money picture yourself having plenty of it, paying bills with ease in a stress-free way or enjoying spending money. You may want to visualize your checkbook with a large balance.

If you want a good relationship picture yourself already in that relationship. You may want to see yourself sharing the normal everyday activities with that person. Allow yourself to enjoy the thoughts and experiences.

As you do this exercise pay attention to your level of comfort. Perhaps you cannot even imagine having what you wish for. Are you editing your dream because you think it unrealistic? Allow yourself to dream. If you will not even allow yourself to dream, it will be almost impossible for your dream to grow and be an actual way of life. Try to imagine visiting a friend or going to work or involved in other activities that are part of your existing routine. Was that difficult? Those things would not happen if you did not think of doing them first. This holds true for a desire that is not yet part of your experience. The tree would never be without the seed.

This concept may be new to you. Give yourself time to get used to it. Push yourself one small step at a time. Slowly add one detail, or a more exciting vision, or a circumstance that is beyond your current experience. You do not have to visualize it all instantly. These slow steps will make the process easier. It will be worth it. Dreaming is important.

Allowing yourself to dream may make you feel uncomfortable at first, especially if you feel it is impossible to have more than you have now. Remember that your only limitations are those set by your own mind. Push through the fear, anxiety, or hesitation, and you will be reprogramming your subconscious to draw in richer experiences.

It is important to note that there is a difference between dreaming and obsessing. Dreaming is a pleasant experience in which you take the time to see yourself, in your mind, with a life full of more meaningful successes. Obsessing is when you cannot *stop* dreaming and it interferes with your life. Dreaming also does not take the place of working to achieve your dreams in your everyday life. Dreaming does allow your vision to take root so that it can begin to grow.

> **Margaret Q.:** Margaret was interested in finding a life partner. The concept of dreaming was new to her, but after several attempts she became comfortable with it. She dreamed of the right relationship and the things she and her partner would do together. Her dreaming made her feel good.
>
> However, after dreaming for several months with no apparent results, she became discouraged. Margaret, it seems, would wake up every morning and spend fifteen minutes thinking about a relationship. Then she would go to work and come home immediately afterward to spend the entire evening dreaming about a relationship. In essence, she made her wish an obsession, so that it

interfered with her life. Dreaming is powerful, but it is not powerful enough to compel a stranger to knock on your door and ask you for a date.

Daring to dream works by sending messages to the subconscious telling it you are ready for something new. The subconscious can then energetically seek out your desire. For this to work you need to live your life, because results occur through people. If you want more money, the money comes through opportunities or people. It does not usually appear on your doorstep in a bag. Margaret isolated herself from people. How could she meet someone when she was home daydreaming all the time?

Finally she limited her dreaming to ten or fifteen minutes a day and otherwise put the relationship issue out of her mind. She resumed her life, went out with friends more often. She met several men and began dating. Three months after she started living her life again, she met someone in line at a deli counter. They started dating and have been together ever since.

So far in this chapter you learned about the power of dreaming. The next step is to learn to fuel your dreams with passion. However, before moving on to learning how to create passion, you must learn how to fine-tune your dreaming in order to fully benefit from it.

The remainder of this chapter will help you to focus your dreams in a healthy, productive way. In order to do this and prepare you for the next step, you must understand the difference between what is called "essence" and "form."

The distinction between these two concepts is crucial when discussing dreaming or visualizing. The "essence" of what you want is conceptual. Essence is closely related to the emotional state you associate with what you want. It is the abstraction of what you want. "Form" is the physical reality of what you want, with all of the specific details. The form of what you want can be experienced through the five senses. The examples below clarify the two concepts.

Examples of Essence:

- I want to be involved in the most correct, permanent relationship for me.
- I want to find a house that will meet all of my needs.
- I want the perfect job for me.
- I want to be accepted into a university that will allow me to learn and grow to my potential.
- I want lifelong financial security.

Examples of Form:

- I want to be in a permanent relationship with John Smith, my accountant.
- I want a promotion to department head.
- I want to live in the house at 52 Green Street.
- I want to win an account with ABC Corporation.
- I want Mary's job.
- I want John and Jane to end their relationship because that would be best for both of them.
- I want to be accepted at Harvard University.
- I want $10,000.
- I want to win the lottery.

When you are defining your dreams, it is best to focus on the essence, rather than the form. There are several reasons for this. First, when you visualize the form of your desires, the major access of power is through the five senses. Your senses only allow visions shaped by past experiences and by familiarity. When you seek the essence of your dreams, you move beyond the limits of the five senses. You can tap into the power of the subconscious which can energetically seek richer experiences, often exceeding what we have known.

Second, focusing on essence (an act of faith and trust that you will be heard) circumvents the desperate, potentially obsessive tone that can be associated with focusing on form: "I want *that* job. I want *that* person." Focusing on essence begins to neutralize the effect of fear, which allows you to expand your comfort zone. Additionally, you could not possibly know the form that all of your options will take. There are infinite possibilities that you may not even be able to imagine. The focus on essence ensures that you pursue dreams that ultimately broaden and enrich your life.

I have learned the hard way to focus on essence. Some time ago I was about to embark on a new project. It was going to cost more money than I had available. I projected, affirmed and visualized (some of those concepts we will be discussing in the next chapter) the exact amount of money that I needed. After a lecture I gave in London, I struck up a conversation with a gentleman who offered me a loan for the exact amount of money I needed. I accepted his offer and initiated my project. This loan, however, had a very specific payback arrangement with a short timetable.

Over the next eight months the pressure caused by the payback arrangement was so great that most of the enjoyment of the project was lost. I was constantly anxious. I was angry with myself for accepting the loan. This experience reinforced for me the importance of working in essence whenever possible. If I had focused on the best possible way to complete my project, rather than limiting my focus to a specific amount of money, I would have found a better way to complete the project while still enjoying the process. My limited thinking and fear about not having the money I needed limited my options.

For many people, focusing on form is based on fear. Fear can drive us to revert back to the limited but familiar visions and desires of the five senses.

You should be aware that focusing on form can be a way to self-sabotage. For example, if you feel you are in love with someone who does not love you and yet you constantly pursue that particular person, you set yourself up for constant rejection. You cannot force someone to love you. By focusing on persuading a person to love you, you limit all other options for a relationship and further strengthen a limiting belief that you do not really deserve love.

It is critical to understand the difference between essence and form. These concepts lay the groundwork for one of the most important principles of the Step-by-Step Method, which is that in dreaming, asking questions, setting goals, working toward your visions, or in reprogramming, your energy and time should be focused only in a positive way, not with the intention of harming, or taking something away from, anyone else.

This idea is important for several reasons. We have emerged from a society in which we were taught that in order for us to win, someone else must lose. We see people around us who believe that their very self-preservation depends on their ability to control others. This concept is self-defeating and self-destructive because it feeds our fears, restricts our options, limits our goals, and sets a process in motion that can turn back on us.

Now that you have learned that the horizon for your hopes and dreams is expansive, it is also apparent that you may not be able to see all of the available possibilities at a specific time, though they do exist. When you dream or focus in such a way as to harm another person, you teach fear and limitation to the subconscious mind in a profound way. Teaching fear undermines your efforts to live a richer, more fulfilling life. Fear is a strong, limiting emotion that counteracts productive work. In addition, when you focus on controlling another, that person can vibrationally sense your desire to control them and learn to distrust you. Attempting to control or harm another person will only hamper your success.

Harm can be accomplished through manipulation, or interfering with another's free will. Free will is a person's right and ability to make his or her own choices. Working to make Jane Smith fall in love with you interferes with her free will. In a five-sensory way, you may not be able to imagine being happy with anyone else but Jane. But, energetically, your subconscious can attract to you what you cannot see. There is no need to limit yourself.

In the final analysis, focusing on the essence of your dreams will be deeply satisfying. Focusing on the form, even when it seems to work and you think a miracle has occurred, may only produce a Band-Aid effect. Focusing on form rarely leads to the kind of change that permanently improves your life.

Occasionally, however, when you need something very specific, working in essence is just not sensible. If you want the perfect object with which to brown bread, it would make sense to ask for a toaster. If you want to possess the correct mode of transportation, asking for a car is just fine. I think the distinction is clear.

The following exercise will take ten minutes. This exercise will help you to make the distinction between essence and form in your life and will show you when it's appropriate to focus on one or the other.

EXERCISE: DID YOU WANT $1,000,000 OR PEACE OF MIND?

Make a list of several very specific things (form) that you would like in your life. For example: a relationship with Jane, winning the lottery, Tom's car.

Take the list and try to turn the desires into essence and see if they make sense. A relationship with Jane can be turned into the most perfect relationship for me. To win the lottery could be a lifetime of financial peace of mind. Tom's car could be the right car.

Review your list. You will see which items make more sense in essence and which in form. It might be easier to become involved with the right person than to try to change Jane and make her the right person. And, believe it or not, it is easier to find lifelong financial peace of mind than to win the lottery or find a bag of money on your door step.

In this chapter you learned the following:

1. Allowing yourself to dream tells your subconscious mind that you are ready to live a richer, more fulfilling life.
2. Dreaming does not replace living and positioning yourself in the world.
3. The essence of your dream is the feeling or emotional state connected to what you want.
4. The form is the physical reality.
5. It is more limiting to focus on form.
6. Focusing on the essence eliminates the possibility of manipulation of others.

Now that you understand the power of your dreams as well as the distinction between essence and form, you are ready for the next step toward taking charge of your life and making your dreams a reality.

6

GOING DIRECTLY TO THE POWER SOURCE

Throughout this book I have described many ways to retrain and reteach the subconscious mind. This chapter will teach you to bypass the most common way of learning—through experience—and to make direct contact with the subconscious mind, with no interference from the ego or conscious mind. When you combine the previous techniques with the techniques from this chapter, you will have the skills and ability to create life experiences limited only by your own imagination.

This chapter is divided into four parts:

1. Visualization
2. Meditation
3. Affirmation
4. Passion

VISUALIZATION

Visualization is the technique of creating a detailed vision or feeling in your mind. It is most effective when used to visualize the effects of the outcome of your desires. The clarity and passion you bring to the process of visualizing will ultimately assure your success.

In Part I we discussed the subconscious mind and its job—making your beliefs a reality. Visualization directly taps into the subconscious part of your mind and gives it new messages. In this way, your own creative force acts as a teacher and parent and creates new beliefs. When you imagine yourself in the position of having what you want, you exude the energy of someone actually in that position. This energy attracts the people and opportunities you need to attain your dreams. It is better to give off the energy of having, rather than of wanting.

Visualization is a very focused form of dreaming. However, the term "visualization" does not mean you are required to actually *see* something. Some people see pictures in their mind, others have a feeling, and some just think. Whatever method is comfortable for you will work just fine. There is no right or wrong way. Purposeful visualization, like anything else, requires practice. It may come to you quite easily or you may have to work on it. Either way, your efforts will be rewarded with miraculous results.

Visualization techniques provide incredible benefits because they allow you to create new, healthier, and more successful patterns. Visualization is the purposeful act of creating the energy, or vibration, of what you would like to attract into your life. We use these techniques all the time, but for many people they are done in an unconscious way that only serves to repeat patterns of the past.

The best way to use visualization is to be clear and focused. Visualization is an extremely effective method for tapping into your subconscious mind. Therefore, it is important to have a plan before you begin. You want to be sure you are sending your subconscious only positive messages.

The following exercise will help you to find a focus. Remember to think about the distinction between essence and form. The exercise will take approximately one hour.

EXERCISE: FINDING A FOCUS

Make a list of things you would like to bring into your life or accomplish within the next thirty days.

Now make a list of things you would like to bring into your life or accomplish within the next six months.

Make a list of things you would like to bring into your life or accomplish within the next year.

Finally, write out where you would like to be in five years.

Now that you have focused on your goals, pick one item from your first list. Relax and begin to visualize the end result of your desire or the task already completed. For example, if you want to be in a relationship, see yourself reading the paper with a partner on Sunday morning, or see some image that represents the level of involvement you want. You may want to visualize yourself receiving a gift or finishing a project. The important thing is to see your particular goal completed. Get in touch with how you will feel once it is accomplished. Allow yourself to experience the full range of emotions that will come with the accomplishment.

You may want to spend a few minutes each day repeating this exercise until you achieve your goal. Sometimes results are instant. Sometimes they take weeks or longer. It all depends on the complexity of what you are asking for. If you change your mind about a particular goal, just acknowledge that you have changed your mind and move on to the next goal.

It is also very positive to visualize your life one or even five years from now, looking exactly as you would want it to.

MEDITATION

The best time to visualize is while in a relaxed, meditative state. Meditation eliminates much of the chatter and influence of the ego. It also bypasses previous learning and makes direct contact with the subconscious—the seat of your beliefs. It is like going directly to a manufacturer rather than to a retailer. Most people find it is easiest to do their visualizations as soon as they wake up in the morning; others prefer just prior to bedtime.

Learning to relax is an important skill. It not only will improve your health but will strengthen your visualizations. Thus, before you focus on visualization itself, it is important to learn to relax. There are a variety of ways to do so. Relaxation is a natural, healthy state that will increase your creativity and productivity throughout the day. Any technique of relaxation that feels right to you will be effective.

To start, put yourself in a relaxed position, either sitting up in a chair with your back perfectly straight or sitting on the floor with your legs crossed. You may also lie down if that will not induce sleep.

Relaxation is easily accomplished by taking slow deep breaths through your nose and exhaling through your mouth. You will begin to calm down automatically. You will feel yourself becoming less tense. After you have spent a few moments focusing on your breathing, visualize yourself slowly walking down a flight of stairs. As you descend, count backward from ten to one.

For many people, just focusing and slowing down their breathing is calming. One of the reasons yoga and other forms of meditation use breathing exercises is that focusing on the breath occupies the ego, and allows you to send messages to the subconscious with less ego interference. Studies have shown that when we are stressed our breathing becomes shallow. When we are relaxed our breathing is deeper, slower, and calmer. By purposefully slowing down and deepening our breathing, we send a direct message to the mind that says we are relaxed. Our body receives the message and relaxes.

Another effective way of relaxing is to focus on relaxing each part of your body in a systematic way. Start your focus on your feet and slowly let the tension leave each muscle. Bring your attention up through your legs and then your body and arms and face. As you focus on each part of your body feel the tension leaving. Relaxing your body while breathing deeply and slowly will put you into a healthy, calm state. We are unaware of how much tension we hold in our bodies. We even hold tension in our faces. As you let the tension leave your body, your deep breathing will feel more and more pleasant.

Sometimes stretching and raising your arms above your head before you begin deep breathing eases the transition to a relaxed state. It will also act as a trigger, preparing your mind for ease.

Another effective way to relax is to listen to a tape of peaceful music or of ocean waves. There are also meditation tapes on the market that can guide you into a relaxed state. Once you have used the tapes several times, relaxing will become so natural to you that you will be able to reach that state readily at any time. The more you practice relaxation, the easier it will become no matter what is happening around you. The ability to relax can be helpful in all sorts of stressful situations. It is easier to make clear decisions in a crisis if you can learn to focus and relax.

Whatever method you use, as you begin to relax, you may feel either that your body is being weighed down or that you are floating. Every experience is different. There is no right or wrong way to feel. It often takes time to quiet your mind, especially when you are first learning to relax. You may want to picture yourself somewhere in nature, or somewhere that feels safe and peaceful. As time goes on, you will find your individual way to reach your place of peace. Do not be discouraged if it takes a lot of practice; it is not easy to relax. With time, relaxation will become part of your routine.

The following exercise can be done whenever you have five minutes during which you will not be disturbed. Having a moment "away from it all" and doing this exercise once or twice a day will lower your stress level, make you calmer, and increase your creativity.

EXERCISE: TIME FOR A FIVE-MINUTE VACATION

Find a place where you will not be disturbed. Sit comfortably in a chair with your feet on the floor and your back straight. Breathe slowly and deeply. With each breath, feel the air filling your lungs. With each exhalation, feel the tension leave each part of your body as all of the air leaves. If you cough when you do this, it is a clear sign that it is an important exercise. Breathing properly will bring in more oxygen, increase circulation, and help your system to function more efficiently. It will also eliminate the excess frenetic energy that you may experience under stress.

Learning to relax at will is a great skill to have.

AFFIRMATION

An affirmation is a verbal way to make a concept firm in your mind. It is a clear statement, as well as a critical way of reprogramming your subconscious to seek out the opportunities you desire. Since everything begins with a thought, the first step in achieving a particular goal is to acknowledge that goal. An affirmation does this in a clear, concise way.

Affirmations are extremely powerful when used with your visualizations. For example, if you are interested in finding a new home, you would relax and visualize the desired outcome for a comfortable amount of time. That could be five minutes or forty-five minutes, whatever feels right to you. When you are finished, make a statement, either in your mind or out loud, that acknowledges the desired outcome of what you have already started to achieve with your thoughts. For example, "I live in the most perfect neighborhood and house for me." You are thus stating your desire as an accomplishment, something that has already been achieved. You are tapping into the feeling of the desired outcome.

Several times throughout the day, you may want to take a slow, deep breath and repeat the affirmation you have attached to the particular visualization. This repetition reinforces your vision.

Pavlov was a Russian scientist who conducted an experiment that involved a dog, a bell, and food. At the same time every day, Pavlov rang a bell just prior to feeding the dog. He did this for months. One day, Pavlov went into the dog's room with no food and just rang the bell. The dog began to produce saliva as if he were in the presence of food. The dog had been conditioned to expect food when he heard the bell and responded physically to the stimulus of the bell.

Repeating an affirmation is analogous to ringing that bell. During the day you may not have time to spend relaxing and visualizing. However, your affirmation will subconsciously trigger the same vibration you create during your visualization. Like the bell, your affirmation should be short and to the point. It should always be phrased positively.

Affirmations have other benefits. Our minds are constantly filled with thoughts. Affirmations replace that chatter. When your mind is filled with chatter rather than with useful, life-enhancing words, negative thoughts about what you can accomplish and what you deserve gain momentum. Affirmations are a powerful tool in combatting the negative "self-talk" that arises from limited beliefs and past experiences.

Just as posing a question first thing in the morning allowed you to play it over and over in your mind during the day until you found the answer, an affirmation will repeat in your mind until the words become a reality in the material world. We need to replace the old thoughts and feelings with ones that are stronger, more favorable, and purposeful.

There are many ways to use affirmations. You can say them silently to yourself in a relaxed state or after a visualization. You can repeat them over and over while you are getting dressed in the morning. This exercise creates excitement, energy, and focus for your desires, and sets the tone for the day. You can sit down and write out the affirmation, including your name and little variations, until you feel the energy and anticipation growing. Think about what you are writing, and begin to feel passion for what you are bringing in with every word.

Find affirmations that feel comfortable to you. Below are a few examples. Each is in essence rather than form. If form feels more appropriate to you, then you make the adjustment.

LOVE:

- I am now involved in a perfect relationship for me.
- I have joy and love in my life.
- I am with my correct spiritual partner.
- I am surrounded by love.

- I am appreciated and loved.
- I radiate light and love.
- I give thanks for the love and support in my life.
- I give and receive love freely.
- I gracefully accept affection and warmth.
- I easily attract loving, caring relationships into my life.
- I love and appreciate myself as I am.
- I am a being of love.
- I enjoy closeness and intimacy with my partner.
- I am completely available to give and receive love.
- I welcome a permanent relationship into my life.
- I open my heart to experience true love and bliss.
- I am part of a loving, giving universe.
- My life is a reflection of universal love.
- I am perfectly aligned with pure joy and love.
- I let go of fear and embrace truth.

MONEY/CAREER:

- I have all the money that I need and want.
- Wealth and riches flow into my life.
- My life is an example of universal abundance.
- Every day in every way I grow richer and richer.
- The universe is completely abundant and my life reflects this abundance.
- I have all that I need and want.
- I hereby accept the wealth of the universe.
- I deserve prosperity and easily embrace it.
- I accept miracles of abundance and opportunity into my life.
- All of my bills are paid and my obligations met.
- I enjoy riches and prosperity every day of my life.
- I am free from financial concerns.
- My life is truly abundant.
- I hereby accept wealth and prosperity as my everyday way of being.
- I have the most perfect job for me.
- Opportunities continually flow into my life.

- I have the most fulfilling career for me and am greatly rewarded.
- The correct career opportunities constantly present themselves.
- I give thanks for my perfect job.
- I love my work and am richly rewarded on all levels.
- I have a career that is deeply rewarding.
- All that I need and all that I want comes to me now.

HEALTH:

- I am in perfect alignment and health.
- I radiate beauty, energy, and health.
- My body reflects universal perfection.
- I give thanks for my perfect health and balance.
- All of my systems are in alignment.
- I am emotionally, physically, and spiritually in balance.
- My body functions perfectly and with ease.
- I am free from pain and physical limitation.
- Everyday I grow healthier and more vital.
- My inner beauty radiates for all to see.
- My mind works to heal my body.
- I let go of illness and embrace health.

SPIRITUAL:

- I am aligned with my highest purpose.
- I radiate love and acceptance for myself and others.
- My life experiences reflect perfect harmony.
- I feel joy and bliss just being alive.
- I am peaceful and serene.
- I love life and life loves me.
- I trust the universe and my path.
- I give thanks for my awareness.
- The universal light shines through me.
- Every day I experience the wonder of the universe.
- I release my past and embrace the truth.
- I am open to the truth.

- I recognize and accept my path.
- Universal light, love, and knowledge shine through me.
- My inner wisdom guides me.
- I live life in perfect correctness and harmony.
- I accept the good in life.
- I am open to my creative energy.
- I embrace love and joy in all I do.
- I see beauty in all.
- I embrace wisdom.

LETTING GO:

- I hereby release my past; I am free.
- I forgive __________ and I give thanks for what I have learned.
- I let go of guilt, pain, and resentments and I embrace love.
- I move forward in confidence and joy.
- I say goodbye to pain, limitation, and fear, and I now live with the light shining through me.
- I am free.

An affirmation that includes the words "I am" serves to align you with your inner strength and life force. It also acknowledges your willingness to take charge of your life, and to accept your deserving all that you need and want. Saying "I am" in a meditation counteracts any messages you might have received, spoken or unspoken, that said you were not good enough. "I am" is an affirmation in itself; it affirms that you are alive and strong and ready to tackle any problem.

"I am" means:

- I am strong.
- I am part of the universe.
- I am loved.
- I am joy.
- I am at peace with myself.
- I am deserving.

- I am free.
- I am radiant energy.
- I am able to love others.
- I am fine the way I am.
- I live.
- I am.

"I am," a simple phrase that you always have with you, can put you in immediate alignment with your highest self. "I am" is a phrase that can free you from anxiety, fear, or doubt. When you say "I am" you will feel connected with your highest purpose. Use this affirmation or find another similar one to achieve this end. Look in your heart and find one that feels right to you. The new words you put together eventually will replace the old tapes you now play in your head.

Kelly F.: Kelly was a walking bundle of nerves. Everything seemed to bother her, from driving in traffic to waiting in line at the supermarket. She tried to create an affirmation that eased the tension and stress she felt almost all of the time. The words "I am" helped a little, but not enough for her to gain acceptance in the everyday trials of life. After identifying the types of situations that gave her the most anxiety, she discovered that her anxiety was strongest in situations that kept her from something. It seemed that on a deep level she was terrified of being abandoned, or missing out on something important if she was late.

She created an affirmation addressing those issues—"It is never too late to have all that I need and want." This affirmation is specific to her needs. She repeats it whenever she feels nervous about being late or waiting. This affirmation has given her peace of mind in situations that used to cause high levels of anxiety.

Jerry Z.: Jerry grew up feeling everything he did was wrong. To combat these feelings he began to lie about activities he participated in or talents he had. As

> he grew older, he felt imprisoned by his habit of lying but was unable to stop. He knew that lying was not necessary, but the habit was deeply ingrained. He tried several affirmations such as "I tell the truth," and "There is no need to lie. I am good enough." These did not have the effect that he desired; he still felt imprisoned by the habit. He rephrased his affirmations to address his particular need—"I release my past. I am free to speak the truth." This affirmation gave Jerry the power he needed to change his habit of lying into one of truth-telling.

If you feel that you cannot have what you are asking for, you may want to pick an affirmation that will help you build a strong foundation, allowing you to acknowledge that you deserve and can have what you ask for.

For example, you may want a permanent relationship but feel on some level that there is no such thing—or that you do not deserve it. Use an affirmation that first addresses the lack of self-worth. For example:

- The perfect relationship exists for me.
- I am ready to embrace a loving relationship.
- I deserve love and happiness.
- I open my heart to love and tenderness.

No matter what you were taught, you do deserve to be happy. No matter what you have done in the past, you deserve love. No matter what anybody says, it is not evil to live prosperously. We are all part of a rich, abundant universe, and we have the right to obtain what we need.

We may not be entitled to the form of what we want, but we are always entitled to the essence. We are entitled to love, peace, health, prosperity, and anything else we need to be happy.

Many of us do not feel deserving. It may seem corny or silly, but for limited attitudes and beliefs to change, you must first affirm that you are deserving, then act "as if" you feel you are entitled. Ask for what you want, even if deep down you do not feel you deserve it. Use your intellect to create a picture of self-confidence and worth. See yourself with all your needs met. Act, speak, and visualize "as if." Eventually your subconscious mind will absorb the new message and view of yourself and your belief system will change.

The following exercise will take less than ten minutes. You may want to do it once a day, or at least several times a week.

EXERCISE:PUTTING IT DOWN IN BLACK AND WHITE

Pick an affirmation that you feel would prove immediately beneficial to you. Write it down at least twenty times. When you are finished, visualize your life as it will be when the meaning of your affirmation becomes a reality. Allow yourself to feel the excitement about what you are creating.

After you are finished visualizing, write out the affirmation one more time. Notice the increased energy you feel. This exercise helps you to focus on what you want.

PASSION

In Chapter 5 I mentioned the importance of passion. Passion is important for several reasons. There are many things you might like to have. A stronger passion for your desires makes them easier to attain. Passion is energy intensified. Energy attracts people and opportunities. Although your thoughts are the first step, it is the passion that energizes and fuels your thoughts that bring your dreams into form.

Passion can be compared to an electric shock. The little shock you feel when you shuffle across a carpet in winter has no major impact. A shock from an exposed electrical socket has a larger one. Your passion determines the energetic impact you make on the world as you pursue your dreams.

When you are working to create what you want, the amount of passion you feel directly correlates to the effectiveness of your visualization. A good way of determining if your visualization is a passionate desire is to see how enjoyable it is to dream about it as a permanent part of your life.

Sometimes finding a positive outlet for passion is tricky. You may be in a situation in which you aren't exactly sure of what you want. You may only be sure that you are unsatisfied with the way things are. Bill, a lawyer, encountered just that problem. He had been working in law for ten years and was not happy. He was tired of his work and felt he would be happier doing almost anything else. To complicate matters, he had no particular interest in any other career. How could he create passion with no focus? Review the following case study and come up with some answers for Bill.

> **Shira B.:** Many years ago I felt I did not have enough money to do the things I wanted to do and was not sure what the next step should be. I knew that I needed to generate a certain income to meet my expenses, and I wanted my work to be inspiring. Like Bill, I was aware that I needed something new but I wasn't sure what.
>
> I decided to access my subconscious mind to help me with this problem. Because I had no specific avenue in mind, I focused on creating passion about the essence of what I wanted, which was an opportunity that was perfect for me. I was not interested in working in an office environment because I needed a sense of freedom, but I needed to earn enough money to cover my living expenses.
>
> I set aside an hour. For the first fifteen minutes I wrote and rewrote the following affirmation. "The most correct opportunity has come to me. I have the perfect job in all ways." During the second fifteen minutes I wrote, "Shira has the perfect job opportunity available. She has the best job she could ever dream of." At this point, I started to feel an optimism, a kind of excitement. For the third quarter of the hour, I wrote "Shira, your job is right for you in all ways. You earn all of the money you could ever need or want. You are inspired by your work. You are completely aligned with your highest purpose."
>
> For the last fifteen minutes I repeatedly stated, "I give thanks for the most correct, perfect job for me. I

immediately have all that I need and want." As I spoke, I varied the words a little, but the feeling was always the same. I said this out loud over and over again, which made me feel excited and extremely optimistic. At one point, it felt so real to me that I wanted to run and tell someone about my new job. I knew that everything was going to be fine. I repeated this exercise twice over the next two weeks. My passion and anticipation grew, until I was looking over my shoulder for someone to run up to me and offer me a job.

Three weeks later I received a call from a friend telling me that a self-improvement lecture was being given at a local Holiday Inn where she worked. The people sponsoring the lecture usually hired ten people for the day to register attendants. As they were short-handed, my friend called to see if I was available. I had never done that kind of work, and it was not something I had the least bit of interest in learning. I went nonetheless.

At the end of the seminar, I introduced myself to the owner of the company. Within minutes we arranged to meet the next day. At our meeting, he hired me to lead seminars for his company. This was an opportunity that I never would have imagined falling into my lap. However, it was the perfect job for me. Within one month, I was happily traveling across the country, leading seminars, feeling fulfilled and inspired, and generating the money that I needed.

Even though the job itself was perfect for me, what was even more important was that this opportunity gave me the exposure and increased confidence I needed as a lecturer. This job positioned me in a place where I could formulate the concept of how I wanted to spend the rest of my working life.

Relate this to Bill. A different strategy was more suited to his personality. Writing to his parents about his achievements had always made him feel proud and happy. With this in mind, he decided to write a letter to his parents, one that he would never send, dated one year ahead. He described his new life and how happy and fulfilled he was in his new career. He thanked them for their love and support during his career change. He made the letter detailed and loving. This process created passion and excitement for him. He did this once a week, each time writing letters, never to be sent, to different friends, giving different details. Five months later Bill had successfully changed careers from law to publishing. His life had become even more satisfying than the descriptions in the letters.

In sparking passion it is helpful to do so in the first, second, and third person. This is because you learn through the ego, the conscious, and the subconscious. You process the things you say to yourself, what others say to you, and what others say about you. This often happens with negative reinforcement. An overweight person has probably overheard people talking about his size. Someone has probably told him directly that he is overweight. At some point he probably tells himself he's fat. Once he begins to send himself this message, he will have a hard time stopping, no matter what actually happens to his weight. Use this knowledge to your advantage. Affirm each of the three perspectives, and you will cover all learning bases.

The next exercise should be completed when you have a lot of time. It should be done with respect and love for your wishes, in private, with no outside influences. This exercise has three parts and may take up to two hours.

EXERCISE:GET READY TO RECEIVE.

1. *Make up categories such as Travel, Career, Health, Education, Relationships, Spiritual Growth, Leisure.*
2. *In each category list things that you would like to have. Do not limit yourself with beliefs of what "cannot be." Just make your list. The act of thinking about what you want is the first step to attaining it. This list is not set in stone. You can modify it as your life and desires change. The act of writing down your desires focuses*

you and allows you to see what you are missing in your life or areas that you would like to improve. This will also put you in touch with the parts of your life that are satisfying to you.

3. *Write a narrative or a letter (that need never be sent) to a friend you have not seen or spoken to in a long time. The letter should be a description of your life as you want it to be. This is a fun and powerful exercise.*

This exercise begins the process of sending focused energy out into the universe. That begins to change your vibrations and thereby attracts opportunities to you.

Visualizations and affirmations can be used at any time you want to make improvements in any area of your life. You can discern the techniques and words that make you feel the most comfortable.

In this chapter you learned:

1. Visualization is the act of creating a vision or feeling in your mind. It is the purposeful act of creating the energy or vibration of what you would like to attract into your life.
2. Relaxation is crucial in order to quiet the ego and gain greater access to the subconscious mind.
3. Affirmations are the verbal route to making a concept firm. An affirmation is a clear statement of a desired outcome.
4. "I am" is a simple phrase that vibrationally aligns you to your highest purpose.
5. Acting "as if" allows the subconscious mind to absorb the new message you are giving it.
6. The level of passion you feel around your desires determines the energetic impact you make.
7. You can create passion even when you are not sure of your focus.

This chapter focused on directly reteaching the part of you that creates and seeks out your life experiences. The next chapter focuses on helping you to identify results.

7

IDENTIFYING RESULTS

When you use the steps in earnest, you will begin to see results—the effects of the visualization and affirmation. Every day you see these effects of your beliefs, whether or not you consciously focus on getting them. If you use the Step-by-Step Method with intention, your results will be favorable.

In some cases, the results will come in ways that you will perceive as coincidental. Some results will feel miraculous. After a while, even the most cynical will become accustomed to results in a variety of forms. When I first began using the Step-by-Step Method to enhance my life, I was so excited I was constantly discussing it with other people. Now favorable results are commonplace, so I keep most of the work to myself and enjoy quiet satisfaction.

The following case studies show several ways that results present themselves:

> **Sandy S.:** Sandy wanted to find a financial backer for her new business, and implemented a visualization routine. She used different steps in this method. She did not see

results fast enough and decided to give up. One afternoon she returned home and listened to her answering machine messages. A girlfriend had invited her to dinner. Sandy accepted. During dinner, Sandy and her friend struck up a conversation with four men sitting at the table next to them. One of the men was in marketing with a venture capital firm. He and Sandy exchanged cards. Although the venture Sandy had in mind was too small for his business, he referred her to a group of doctors who invested in small businesses as partners. After several meetings, Sandy and the investment group struck an agreement to do business.

Hal R.: Hal had been wanting to lose weight for years. He had tried many diets but always had been unsuccessful. He then used the Step-by-Step Method to reteach his subconscious mind to become attracted to healthier foods. Since Hal anticipated a precipitous weight loss, he at first became discouraged by the Step-by-Step Method because he did not see dramatic results. Some six months later and fifty pounds lighter, he realized that results happen in a healthy, natural way. Results happen through people and through our own attitude and behavior changes. They occur in the most correct way possible.

Maryanne B.: Maryanne was in love with Jeff from the moment she met him. She could not imagine being happy with anyone else. He, unfortunately, did not feel the same way. He wanted their relationship to be a friendship and nothing more. She faithfully created the flow and visualized for four months. Their friendship grew into a stronger friendship, but not into a romantic relationship.

Maryanne felt frustrated and stuck. Her dilemma? She could not visualize a relationship without seeing Jeff, yet she was aware of the dangers in focusing on form. Her solution? Maryanne visualized a perfect relationship with passion and desire. She allowed Jeff's image to float through her mind. She ended her visualization, however, with the affirmation "This or something better now comes into my life." By amending her visualization with the affirmation she told her subconscious mind that she was willing to meet and become involved with someone who was correct for her.

Two months later she met another man for whom she developed an attraction. They began to date. Jeff did not immediately leave her thoughts, or even her dreams, though it did begin to happen slowly. In the meantime, she began developing a loving relationship with a man who appreciated, and wanted to be with, her. Her new situation has transcended the relationship she imagined she would have with Jeff.

You cannot force yourself to abandoned feelings for someone. You can, however, use the passion you feel, directing it with an affirmation in a healthy, noncontrolling way. Attempting to interfere with someone else's free will, as Maryanne had initially tried to do with Jeff, will not produce the results you want. It will, in fact, feed your frustrations.

Dennis C.: Dennis works as an engineer in a small, competitive firm. He was jealous of his co-workers' successes, even though he had many of his own. He continually felt that their coups detracted from his, making him a less valuable employee. He radiated jealousy and fear. This fear made it more difficult for him to work with the others, resulting in a performance level that began to slip.

He began creating the situation he feared most: not being good enough. He knew that he had to make a change and so attended a lecture on the Step-by-Step Method. Dennis initially focused on improving the six habits that were described in Chapter 4. This allowed him to get off the treadmill of fear. He is now back on track, and keeps his jealousy and insecurity at bay through affirmations.

These examples of successful results bring up the concept of plenty. As you begin to incorporate the Step-by-Step Method into your daily thinking and life, you will know that someone else does not have to lose for you to win. There is no need for jealousy, manipulation, or control. There is enough in the universe. You will have enough. This is not to say that some people are not at a disadvantage at the outset. But in every society and every situation, there are people who accomplish what others would call the impossible. They leave bad neighborhoods, they recover from a fatal illness, or they make something of their lives with no outside help at all. People with these kinds of accomplishments had a vision or dream for themselves. They found a way to make something of their lives, even though initial prospects appeared bleak.

A talent or a beauty that someone else possesses has nothing to do with you or your abilities. It does not mean that you have less. It is quite common to feel jealous and to find fault when an attractive person walks into a room. This critique somehow makes the criticizer feel better. She fears being perceived as less desirable in comparison. In fact, she is less desirable; that type of pettiness radiates fear and jealousy which is unattractive to most people on every level. This fear stems from a belief that there is not enough beauty—or other positive traits—to go around. It is also based on the belief that physical beauty is the only thing others are attracted to. Appreciating beauty as well as exhibiting self-confidence makes you more attractive. Working in confidence and love makes a statement, gives off a welcoming vibration and creates positive results.

On another note, just because you experience a result does not mean it is *the* result. Throughout your life you continually send messages and energy out into the universe. You do this both consciously and unconsciously. It is important to remember that when you begin dreaming and visualizing in a focused way, you may still experience results from energy output created during an earlier period of your life—phantom results.

Using the Step-by-Step Method you will begin to see immediate results. But your initial results may or may not be the ones you have been focusing on most recently.

You may assume that what immediately comes into your life is a result of your most recent visualization and that it is for your highest good. However, you must use your common sense and your intuition. Your first few results may just be examples of the energy beginning to move. Your desired results will come. Do not settle for something unless it matches or exceeds the essence of what you want. You must trust your healthiest feelings. The following case study is an example of a phantom result.

> **James T.:** James wanted a new job. He began visualizing the perfect job that met all of his needs. One week later an old friend called to tell him there was a job posting in his department that seemed right for him. James sent his résumé and interviewed for the position. During the interview it became clear that the position was not what he was looking for. He did, however, receive a job offer. James felt confused. He had visualized and affirmed to attract the right job. Within a week a friend had called him out of the blue to tell him about one. Now he was offered the position! This sounded like the results of a visualization, but it did not *feel* right.
>
> James trusted his intuition and turned down the job offer, continuing to visualize and affirm. It was another three months before a new opportunity presented itself. During those months, James wondered if he had made a mistake and had "looked a gift horse in the mouth." Eventually, a new job became available in the company where he worked. It turned out to be exactly what he wanted. James was offered this job, and was grateful that he had waited for the right result.

The first opportunity is not always the right one. As visualization and purposeful reteaching become a way of life for you, you are less likely to have many phantom results, results of energy moving but without the final outcome you wished for. To illustrate this point, think of a hose that has a clog in the middle of it. Your visualization will act as the water going through the hose.

The first thing out will be the clog. The clog may be old thoughts or energies you placed in the hose long ago. The clog may also be what you need moved in order to be aligned with what you want.

People are always concerned with time frames. "How long will it take?" There is no set answer. Sometimes the results are instant. Sometimes they take months. In more complicated visualizations, there are a lot of pieces that need to fall into place before you experience the end result. Most of us feel impatient as we begin the process of change. Be patient with yourself and remember that you are changing a lifetime of habit.

Remember, just because you cannot measure progress with your five senses, that does not mean there is no activity. You cannot see a thought, but it is where everything begins. Just have faith.

Throughout this book it has been explained that your conditioning and many of your life experiences stem from your childhood and learned self-esteem. It has also been explained that you do not have to fall victim to your past for your entire life. You can at any moment change your present and your future.

Your past may have created anger, as well as negative patterns that are difficult to change. Each and every time you re-create a pattern from your past, you not only feel the sadness of what you are doing today, but also the sadness from the time when you had no choice but to accept the pattern.

Anger must be experienced before you can let go of it. It is unrealistic to think you can keep hiding it away. There may be patterns you are not ready to let go of. Do not mentally punish yourself for that. Acknowledge that you are not ready, and that you will let go when you are. Take notice that you are re-creating patterns and learned behaviors. You will let go when the time is right. You will free yourself. No one else can tell you the time that is right for you.

The Step-by-Step Method can help with any area of your life. It is important to keep in mind, however, that certain issues are deep and painful. To resolve these issues it will be helpful to have support in your efforts.

You can make a change in your life no matter what your situation is. We all have expectations of how we want changes to occur. There are specific outcomes we desire. As you begin this work, you may not know what is the most correct thing for you. Focus on essence, and trust that a source higher than you does know.

I have wished for specific things that I never received. I have also, however, received things that were beyond what I ever had imagined. Leave yourself open for more than you can visualize. You can do this by affirming after your meditations "this or something better now manifests for me."

Allow yourself to live life with love and joy and abundance. This is not always easy. You may have to reteach yourself. You may have to redefine your values. Be fearless in letting go of your past conditioning. Embrace and enjoy a new life.

In this chapter you have learned the following:

1. Results present themselves in natural ways that at first you might be tempted to call coincidences.
2. Phantom results are from energy moving, but are not the final outcome.
3. Anger must be experienced before you let it go.
4. You need to be patient with yourself in this time of change.

You now have most of what you need to know to change your life from the inside out. You know how to identify results. Have fun with the process. Do not make your dreams and wishes an obsession. Make your affirmations and visualizations a part of your life, not your whole life. This work is meant to help you experience greater joys, successes, victories, and love in your life. It is not meant to take the place of your life.

Part III will help you to fine-tune your thinking, further aligning you with passion, excitement, and the readiness to embrace joy.

Part III

FINDING FREEDOM

8

A NEW WAY OF LIFE

In Part I, you built a strong foundation for change. You discovered the way you think, learn, experience, and process information. In Part II, you uncovered the techniques that will help you consciously benefit from that knowledge, and you discovered how to implement and embrace the changes you have learned to create. Part III is dedicated to taking all that you have accomplished and learned one step further. You will address ways of thinking that do not promote growth, and learn to replace them with healthier concepts. This will promote the living of life, not only in the absence of pain but in real joy and abundance.

Using the Step-by-Step Method you can correct any problem that arises. If you are short of money, you can use your own internal power to attract an opportunity to generate income. If you are lacking motivation, you can "affirm" yourself into an energetic state. If you are without focus, you can ask your computerlike mind to direct you. You have incredible resources available to you at every moment. You have access to unlimited opportunities and potential.

This problem-solving ability that you now have is a wonderful tool; however, the real gift is received after the crises are over and your life feels manageable. This is the time when the miracles of freedom and joy occur. Life is not meant to be a series of catastrophes to recover from, fires to put out, and people to conquer. Life can be an ecstatic expression of joy and love.

In the past, this concept may have felt completely foreign to you. You may then have thought your life experiences came about through luck, either good or bad, or a series of coincidences. Now you know that it is your subconscious mind that has created them. You also know that you can greatly improve your life through reteaching your subconscious mind.

The remainder of this chapter will address subtle but powerful concepts that will further awaken you to higher levels of self-awareness and growth. Knowledge of these concepts will enable you to fully integrate all that you have learned and accomplished.

The following five concepts will assist you in this final step toward your dreams:

1. Responsibility
2. Absence of Pain
3. Desire
4. True Identity
5. Deserving and Respect

RESPONSIBILITY

Being responsible for your life is not about blaming yourself. It is also not about blaming others. Being responsible is the act of fearlessly looking at your life and identifying events or situations that may have harmed you in some way, events or situations that served as a teacher to your subconscious. If your mother was controlling, your early relationship with her may have started a pattern of energetically seeking out the same type of woman as a partner in business or life. Taking responsibility is not about blaming yourself for seeking out unhealthy relationships or blaming your mother for causing this to be part of your life.

Taking responsibility is admitting what happened to you, no

matter how painful, and acknowledging that it is now up to you to free yourself from this pattern. It is not up to your mother. Just as you cannot change her, she cannot change you. Your mother cannot "fix" it. Holding on to the anger will not fix it, nor will blaming her. Taking responsibility for claiming your life and reteaching yourself not only will free you from the past, but will allow you to forgive yourself and her. The anger you feel stems from unresolved issues and blame. Forgiveness alleviates that anger.

Freeing yourself is not about holding back feelings or denying the pain or anger. It is about making the decision to pay the price to reteach your subconscious. Paying the price can be identified by:

1. Fearlessly facing the past and how it may have hurt you.
2. Coming to terms with the fact that only you can change your future and no one can do it for you.
3. Admitting that you do not have to be a victim.
4. Facing your fears.
5. Identifying your role in perpetuating the original learning through adult choices.

In order for you to improve an area of your life, you must identify what went wrong. In order to repair something, you must know what is broken. It is important to know that you may experience anger or rage during the identification process. That is normal. It may be helpful to create a support system for yourself, either through therapy or friends.

Once you have identified the specific dynamics, it is your job to understand that although the initial experience was not your fault, it is your responsibility to free yourself from it in order to change your present and future. You will not be a victim of your past once you take responsibility for your future.

Taking responsibility subtly changes the vibration that you put out and acts as a beacon to other people. During the vibrational change from denying responsibility to accepting it, you may experience a lull in events in the affected area of your life, a break in activity during the shift in attitude and awareness. After a while, the subconscious mind will send out the message that you are ready to draw in new experiences, experiences that are not reflective of past events and beliefs. The lull before this happens is best described by the next concept.

THE ABSENCE OF PAIN

There are those who have spent much of their lives with one problem or crisis after another. For them, the absence of pain feels like ecstasy. They wish for the absence of pain rather than happiness because that is the limit of what they can imagine.

After the initial relief from pain, anxiety can set in. People feel anxious because this new place of peace is unfamiliar. In many cases they sabotage the plateau because of the newness of the condition. They may feel that the situation is too good to be true. They may have that feeling of impending doom. The waiting for some may be intolerable. Another experience may be boredom. They are used to the high energy or "chaos" of problems, so that the lack of the same makes them feel restless. They look for an outside event, something familiar with which to fill the void.

A wise man, Baba Muktananda, made a beautiful distinction between pleasure and joy. "Pleasure depends on outside stimuli and has a beginning and an end. Joy does not depend on outside stimuli and has no beginning and no end. Pleasure is human, and joy is divine." The absence of pain is the plateau, or resting place. It provides an opportunity for you to reap the benefits of hard work and to gear up toward profound internal changes.

Using the Step-by-Step Method, the state of joy can be reached. We know that we cannot change or control other people, that expecting other people to render us happy or make everything okay is unrealistic. We also know that fear hurts us and interferes with our happiness. With all that we have learned, we know that we can find our happiness within, and can create a reality that reflects this happiness. At first, striving for pleasure is powerful and validating. But as the true power within is realized, the ability to experience joy is unveiled.

In the past, this concept of joy, or looking inward to find happiness rather than blaming—or focusing on—others, may have felt completely foreign to you. Now that you have tapped into your internal energy and you know there are countless options and opportunities, being truly happy can be one of these. You always have the choice.

Use your own internal power to alleviate crises in your life. Use your focus and visualization to attract all that you need. Internalize and recognize that you always have other options. Feel yourself letting go of situations, conditions, and relationships that are harmful to you, knowing that there is something better. Your past does not have to parallel your future.

Finding a way to be comfortable in the absence of pain, or during the lull before new results can be felt, requires faith. It also may take some time, depending on the size and quality of the change. True desire speeds up the process. It may take a day, a week, a month, or longer. Each person is different, and experiences his or her results in a different way.

DESIRE

This concept of desire is not a new one. It is a common link that aids in changing the future for all people. If you recall, you are only limited by your own ability to dream, wish, or desire. Allow yourself to dream, acknowledge your desires, and fuel your life with passion. As you begin this process you may feel resistance to acknowledging a desire that is beyond your previous experience. You may also hear and feel resistance from people around you.

Some people in your life have a stake in your stagnation. The reason is that as you change, it shakes their belief system of what is possible. They may be fearful for you and try to hold you back. They may rely solely on what they can experience through the five senses and expect you to do the same. As you change, it also puts them in touch with their own attitudes and level of responsibility. For these reasons they may try to push you to reevaluate or question your desire.

For many, the act of taking responsibility is frightening. It is much easier to blame others. As you express your desires and start seeing results it may bring up dissatisfactions in those around you. Do not let their doubts, fears, and insecurities hold you back. You cannot change them. Work on yourself. As you change, you will act as an inspiration to others. As you form a new identity for yourself, through your own strength, you will then draw in new people and experiences to fit the new you. This brings you to the next concept.

TRUE IDENTITY

We tend to identify ourselves by what we do and what we have. Who we are has nothing to do with our job, how much we make, our possessions, or the success of our children. We are simply who we are. These outside events make up some of the details of our lives. That is all.

If you were stranded on a desert island without any of your possessions, you would still be you. If you changed jobs or entered a monastery, you would still be you. Only the details of your life would change. The quality of your ability to love, give, and receive, to show compassion, support, and understanding are with you always and are closer to who you are than the clothes you wear. It is easy to identify yourself by things measurable through the five senses. Clearly, you are more than that.

This superficial identification process can just as easily be linked to your traumas and failures. During workshops it is quite common to hear people gleefully giving voice to a shopping list of trials and tribulations, clearly implying that this is who they are, or what makes them special.

When you decide to change your identification from an external condition to an internal condition, you gain a new and wonderful freedom and security. Outside events change constantly in ways that you have no control over. Economies change, people come in and out of your life. Your internal identity cannot be touched by others, or society or the economy. Your internal peace of mind can remain intact. This makes it easier to handle day-to-day happenings. If you build your identity on the amount of money you make, what happens if the economy turns, and you are making less or none at all?

When your identity is based on a changeable circumstance, such as salary, being a doctor, or living in a certain neighborhood, perceptions are dramatically altered when a change occurs. If you identify yourself with the neighborhood you live in, and circumstances require you to move, you will not only feel the normal sadness of moving but you will also feel as though your world is coming to an end. The decision to move, no matter how correct, will be an almost impossible one because it touches on your false identity.

When your false identity is challenged you experience what is commonly known as someone "pushing your buttons." Having your buttons pushed is a direct challenge or affront to your insecurities. Feelings of insecurity or nervousness about your ability to take care of yourself financially can be exacerbated by a parent's offhanded comment that you never seem to make any money. Such a comment can cause anger, resentment, doubt, and fear, and can plague your thoughts.

A button-pushing comment may be quite subtle, and still create the same feelings. If you have been struggling with your weight and a friend or family member comments at dinner that they see you are on a diet "again," this can also feel like an assault.

In either of these scenarios, if you felt secure or did not overly identify with the issue, you might have been slightly irritated or have felt unsupported—or nothing at all. The comment would not have plagued or overwhelmed you.

DESERVING AND RESPECT

Understanding the differences between essence and form makes the concept of deserving easier to accept. In essence, we all deserve to have what we need. This is not a selfish concept. Who we are and how we behave, directly affects those around us and indirectly affects the people who associate with them. When you understand that you should be treated with respect and that you deserve to be happy, you can then take care of yourself. When you take care of yourself in a respectful way, you take care of those around you. The following is a list of the most common ways people harm others while not taking care of themselves.

1. When a person does not leave an abusive marriage, the children are harmed.
2. When an alcoholic does not seek treatment, everyone around him is harmed.
3. When people do not see to it that they get enough rest, they do not perform as well at work, and their co-workers are harmed.
4. When a person does not allow others to give to him or her, he or she robs friends of that joy.
5. When a person's health is not taken care of, the lives of family members are disrupted.
6. When a person does not state needs in a relationship, the other partner is set up for failure.
7. When a person is not honest with a friend, that friend does not have the knowledge that could help him or her.

These are just a few examples. The list is infinite. If you do not feel you deserve to be happy and prosperous and cared for, it will be difficult to treat yourself with true respect. When you do not treat yourself with respect, those around you suffer as well. We are all part of the same universe. If we compare it to a pool of water, each and every drop that makes up the pool affects the quality of the water itself. Each one of us is a drop of water. Each and every drop that goes into the pool affects every other drop, and slowly affects and changes the pool itself. So, you must approach your every desire with respect and love. You are not in a vacuum, you are not alone. In respecting yourself and your wishes, you create a beauty and strength that promotes love and change for all.

Unlike those moments in cooking, when you find you have to run out to the store for missing ingredients, life does not require last-minute shopping. You already have inside you all the ingredients you'll ever need. The Step-by-Step Method can be used anywhere with no props or outside help. You have all that you need, just as you are, to be happy, successful, or anything you choose; for these things do not depend on the economy, your friends, your spouse, your boss, or any outside force. You have the strength and you have the power—right now—to be successful, prosperous, and joyous.

AFTERWORD

We are in a time of expansion and creativity. We have access to information that can lead us to pure enlightenment. Enlightenment is not just a concept, it is freedom. It is freedom to overcome the past, freedom to improve the quality of our lives, freedom to live prosperously, as well as freedom to love others and ourselves unconditionally.

It is time to embrace our power through peace, love, and joy in our every waking moment.

ABOUT THE AUTHOR

Shira Block is a specialist in the field of human potential. She has been teaching personal and spiritual growth and awareness since 1985. Shira has traveled throughout the United States, Canada, and England, conducting workshops and seminars. In her private practice, located in Massachusetts, she specializes in personal empowerment, motivation, stress reduction, spiritual growth, habit changing, increasing self-esteem, and making dreams a reality.

THE SAGE SERIES

The Sage Series offers guided meditation tapes to induce a deep meditative state.

Meditation tapes currently available:

Be Your Perfect Weight

Increase Motivation

Increase Your Psychic Abilities

Live Stress Free

Create Your Life (Manifesting Your Dreams)

Relaxation

Health and Body Alignment

Prosperity

Individualized meditation tapes made on request for health, wishes, and personalized work.

Private and group appointments, classes, and workshops are available. For more information, to schedule appointments, to sponsor a workshop or seminar, or to order tapes write to:

SHIRA BLOCK
PO Box 1026
Northampton, MA 01061

SUGGESTED READING

You Can Heal Your Life, Louise L. Hay

Seat of the Soul, Gary Zukav

Ageless Body, Timeless Mind, Deepak Chopra, M.D.

The Kyballion, Three Initiates

Living in the Light, Shakti Gawain